MOVING MOUNTAINS
BY FAITH

Moving Mountains By Faith
Copyright © 2022 by CAROLYN VAN LOH

Published in the United States of America
ISBN   Paperback: 978-1-959761-41-9
ISBN   eBook: 978-1-959761-42-6

All rights reserved. No part of this publication may be reproduced, stored in a retrieval system or transmitted in any way by any means, electronic, mechanical, photocopy, recording or otherwise without the prior permission of the author except as provided by USA copyright law.

The opinions expressed by the author are not necessarily those of ReadersMagnet, LLC.

ReadersMagnet, LLC
10620 Treena Street, Suite 230 | San Diego, California, 92131 USA
1.619. 354. 2643 | www.readersmagnet.com

Book design copyright © 2022 by ReadersMagnet, LLC. All rights reserved.

Cover design by Jacob Van Loh
Interior design by Daniel Lopez
Photo used by permission of "The Globe of Worthington, MN".

MOVING MOUNTAINS
BY FAITH

CAROLYN VAN LOH

ReadersMagnet, LLC

Table of Contents

Acknowledgements From The Author vii
Introduction xi

Chapter 1 1
Chapter 2 7
Chapter 3 10
Chapter 4 18
Chapter 5 24
Chapter 6 34
Chapter 7 46
Chapter 8 54
Chapter 9 58
Chapter 10 64
Chapter 11 69
Chapter 12 76
Chapter 13 82
Chapter 14 89

Author's Biography 99

Acknowledgements from the Author

The "seed" for this book originated from a Tyler High School assignment. Each student chose individual projects of interest, and I chose to write about the biography of my family. Mom and Dad evidently helped me because there were interesting facts that I could not remember. Thank you, Mom and Dad, for overseeing me so I could record special facts about our family when I was a teen.

Family, close family friends and others willingly contributed to this book. My husband Dave tops the list of those supporting me working on this labor of love. I wrote and published in 2013 the little book *A Place of Interest*, based on his mother Betty's diaries. I used week-at-a-glance calendars where she kept records for appointments, activities, etc. and then included farm life activities and a few family facts.

I don't have the luxury of a stack of writings from Mom or Dad like my mom-in-law's calendar/journaling; however, I have had the responsibility using a stack of documents and newspaper clippings I used to glean and verify facts. Dad's memoir notes from his WWII experiences gave me an added dimension of his military years, times not readily talked about to us children.

Daniel Norgaard, my second cousin, has spent time conducting personal interviews and researching Norgaard family histories online. He graciously printed copies of a wealth of his collected information that I used concerning the Don Norgaard family history. Finally, I understand why a large Norgaard family tree has my great grandfather's photo in one corner and the other corners contain photos of his three wives. No wonder the family tree configuration always puzzled me as I walked past it daily. Now I understand the unusual family tree relationships.

Larson family information originated with my Great Aunt Anna (Larson) Trimble who began writing. "My Family History" during the summer of 1926 when attending summer school at the University of Minnesota. She was a dear lady. Knowing now that she was a teacher, I can understand why I enjoyed her during her retirement years when she came to visit my mom, her niece Ada. My cousin Bob Dwire's wife Oda used Aunt Anna's family tree information, updated information and included selected photos in 1991.

I appreciate information contributed by my siblings and their families, my childhood neighbors Dennis Blomgren, David Guida and his wife provided a home for Mom and Dad after the Norgaard foreclosure, cousins Keith Dwire and his sister Sharon Sannerud, and deceased Rev. Wayne Anderson's written eulogy of Don. A special thank you to my first proofreader, Rachel Hanson, a pastor's wife and English teacher who also has similar writing interests I enjoy. Jacob Van Loh, one of Don and Ada's great grandchildren, designed this book's front cover. Thank you, Jacob!

A never-ending story has begun. Which generation will take the responsibility of bringing this story up to date, if possible, a few decades ahead?

Carolyn Norgaard Van Loh.

Introduction

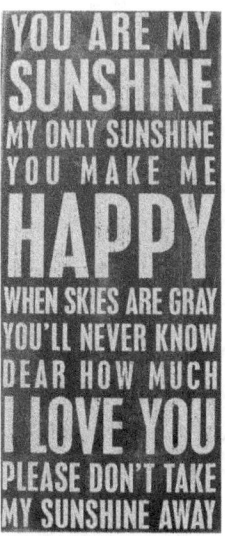

> *Don sang this song while driving his John Deere home at the end of the day.*

My dad, Don Norgaard, shared with me the following Bible verses three days prior to God calling my mom, Ada, home to Heaven August 5, 2001. "I tell you the truth, if you have faith and do not doubt, not only can you do what was done to the fig tree, but also you can say to this mountain, 'Go, throw yourself into the sea,' and it will be done. If you believe, you will receive whatever you ask for in prayer" (Matt. 21:21 & 22 – NIV).

Dad told me that the verses had been helpful to him and Mom for a long time. He was overwhelmed with the impending final good-bye to his beloved wife of nearly 60 years when he shared with me the faith as Jesus explained to His followers.

Faith means daily dependence on God but is not intended to help us avoid big problems because God is still in control.

Dad and Mom practiced their faith in God as they experienced numerous mountainous challenges over the years of their daily living. Reading about our family in the heritage chapter reveals portions of stories when Danish and Norwegian ancestors faced life's major challenges when bringing family members from Europe to the USA. Problems such as health and economic conditions in Europe motivated our ancestors who emigrated to America.

My faith in God has guided me to assemble and record the challenging experiences for their progeny.

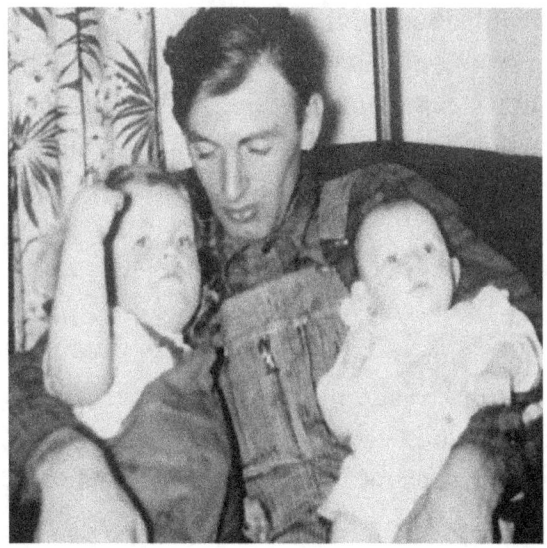

Don loved his little girls Carolyn (left) and Valerie (right) after a busy day.

Life is full of mountainous challenges. Reading about Mom and Dad's families, ancestors will demonstrate how their forerunners faced challenges. Mom and Dad's story is divided into chapters dealing with their life's challenges. Most of the information was collected over a period of several years, but it wasn't until March 2020 when developing this story became my priority, thanks to the Covid-19 Pandemic changing this author's daily schedule.

A couple years before Mom died, I gave her and Dad special diaries that were arranged as yearly calendars. Each day provided questions for them to answer about their family history, their education and other interesting topics. Some of their answers are recorded in this story. Dad became lonely when Mom could not live in their apartment because of health conditions, so I gave Dad a writing assignment that can be called a memoir of his military experiences during WWII. Deciphering his penmanship, spelling, and English grammar were a challenge for me, but I was impressed with what he wrote because most of his comments were memories that I had never heard him share with me.

Dad's "Battery B" members had twenty-six reunions in nearly a dozen states from 1972-1997. As I was compiling information for this story, I remembered the few times my husband and/or I drove Mom and Dad to these reunions and met several of the men and their wives. I wish now I had asked these men more about their military experiences.

Photo of little Donald Brodson Norgaard

Writing this book was like assembling a challenging jigsaw puzzle. My story of Mom and Dad came together piece-by-piece until the entire story began developing. Some of the facts and details were hard to find, but I diligently continued searching until the story developed, like a jigsaw puzzle lacking a couple pieces, Mom and Dad's birth dates December 24, 1917, and November 28, 1918, occurred as World War I battles were decreasing, and the Spanish Flu Pandemic would soon be over. Experiencing the Great Depression as teenagers was another challenging way that would have been an interesting story to share with younger Norgaard family members; however, my parents didn't talk much about their historic era. Dad occasionally discussed farming the dry lakebed of Lake Benton as a teenager during drought years of the 1930s.

NOTE: This story's chapters are arranged according to subjects discussed, not in chronological order.

The term Don refers to a soldier and Dad means post-army stories.

Chapter 1

December 7, 1941:
"a date which will live in infamy."

Don left his special car behind when he enlisted in the military.

Pearl Harbor's attack motivated the USA military to swing into high gear for battle. Potential soldiers were energized and prepared to be ready.

The foundation of Dad's life had been completed before this attack quickly changed Dad and Mom's lifestyle adventure.

Dad, a farmer at heart, grew up on a farm and was a good gardener who loved working there. 4-H club membership records and photos showcased his accomplishments. Minnesota 4-H honored him with trips, one to Duluth and another to a 4-H gathering in Minneapolis. Friend and employer Jean Blomgren penned Dad's various talents in poetry and wrote for Mom and Dad's 25th wedding anniversary celebration.

He always could raise the best of everything:

Tomatoes and melons by the bushel he'd bring.

I remember the many days a dozen he'd eat.

But never an inch did it add to his waist or seat.

Then came the day he left home to work for others.

There were many experiences, some good and some oh, brother!

Each year some new knowledge he did

Bible School showing Arco area children at District 18 school. Ada is in front second from left, brother Gordy is in back second from right.

That has helped through the years again and again.

In 1941 Dad was a hired hand at the Myron and Jeanne Blomgren farm on State Highway 19 northeast of the small community of Arco which connected Dad and Mom when she lived with her sister May and husband Roy Dwire on their farm a short distance from their good friends. Mom and Dad easily became friends, even to the point of considering marriage. I once asked Mom what she and Dad did for weekend dating activities. If they had money, Mom said they would attend a movie theater; no money, they attended Sunday evening services at First Baptist Church in Tyler. They liked the Danish immigrant pastor, Rev. J.R. Brygger. Mom knew him from his summer Bible School tent meetings at the country school where she and her siblings attended school. She learned about faith in God as a result of Brygger's preaching and teaching.

Her dad Chris also attended the tent meetings and became a friend of Rev. Brygger. He later told the family he desired having Rev. Brygger conduct his funeral when the day came. Providentially, his Lutheran minister was out of state for a church conference when Chris breathed his last breath, so the family had no problem about inviting Brygger to conduct the memorial sermon. This Danish minister had enjoyed visiting the Larsen family at their farm. Mom was a senior in high school when her dad died.

The Blomgrens and Dwires were the unofficial matchmakers for Mom and Dad, and Jean wrote about the budding romance in one of her poems.

While Don was working for Roy, Ada he met at a party, Who was really bashful, rosy-cheeked, healthy and hearty.

Shy as they were, their hearts started to pound; Until a date from each other they had found.

Don had promised Roy

That he was a saving boy, And his money he wouldn't need Until spring or time to seed.

But come the second month of the year, He asked Roy for some money—with fear, Then an explanation was due without doubt, And Roy recorded he paid Don to take Ada out.

Both were the quiet type and wanted no one to know, But these things have a way of getting out.

While working on this story, I discovered a few of Dad's letters dated "1940". Their available communication options were quite sparse compared to devices used sixty years later The seed of romance was planted.

Letter writing between Dad and Mom began early in their relationship and continued during WWII. I confess, as an adolescent, I snooped in one of Mom's dresser drawers and found some potentially valuable letters from Dad that had portions of the letters clipped out! He was writing from the military! Hoping to do more reading, the next time I snooped, all the letters were gone.

Jean B. penned, "Ada waited for her mail be it sunshine or rain. Many letters would be fun to read but bet we don't—that would be a bad deed."

In a collection of "leftover" papers and collectables found in my possession, a couple of Dad's hand-written letters from 1940 were revealing. From the comments made by Dad, he and Mom wrote regularly, even though Dad worked nearby Mom at the Ralph and Erma Madden farm. Below are a few typical comments indicating Dad's personality and sense of humor.

Sunday, April 7, 1940 he wrote: "Your letter writing is improving, keep up the good work. I really do look forward to them."

"It's getting so that it is almost work for me to sit down. Been riding the tractor until I have calluses on my sitter. Guess I'll have to get a soft pillow."

"Good night, pleasant dreams, and don't let the bedbugs bite. My sincerest love, Don" (ending with a swirl on the "n" of his name.)

In an April 21, 1940, letter he wrote, "I left my mustache on when I shaved this morning. Mrs. Madden [his boss Ralph's wife] says they'll be asking me which circus I belong to."

"It seems queer, doesn't it, that everybody is so concerned with our affairs. Let's hope that it makes them feel happier because it certainly doesn't bother us. Does it?"

"We'll be looking forward to next weekend together, unless you hear to the contrary. With my best love, Don."

The Japanese attack on Pearl Harbor in Hawaii was just the incentive needed for the young couple, so they immediately determined they must get married before he joined the military.

Chapter 2

December 25, 1941: Wedding Bells

| Don and Ada Norgaard wedding photo |

Wedding plans were in the making
When Uncle Sam did start taking
All the young men our country did call,
And Don answered the call—very straight and tall.
But before he did have to go,
He knew he'd be a lonely GI Joe.
It'd help to know his love he could see,

> *Don was quick to enlist in the army when Pearl Harbor was attacked and the wedding date was set immediately.*

So, Ada consented a war bride to be.

Jean Blomgren

Don and Ada's 4 p.m. wedding was one-of-a-kind because of the circumstances, starting with the date they chose. His farmer-boss family, the Myron Blomgrens, were planning to be gone over Christmas, so they asked Don to stay at the farm, milk the cows and keep everything running smoothly. Don's brother Arnold and fiancé Fern Elbers were the attendants for the December 25 wedding ceremony at Bethany Lutheran Church in nearby Arco, Minnesota. The pastor and his wife were the only other people attending.

After the wedding vows, the two wedding party couples drove back to the Blomgren farm and finished the chores before driving to the Atlantic Hotel in Marshall for their wedding dinner.

The newlyweds received typical wedding gifts from friends and family. Don's parents and their attendants were the only ones to give a gift on the wedding day. The rest of the gifts arrived during January. Money gifts were often the amount of $1; the groom's parents gave $10. Other gifts were like contemporary wedding gifts: kitchen linens and utensils, bedding, and a recipe book. [The gift list was listed in the couple's wedding record book.]

In one of Dad's memoirs he wrote, "When I was about to go and be inducted, I think both Ada and I cried most of the night. We did not know if we would ever see each other again. War was war, and we were a part of it now for better or worse. How precious those moments were! From then on, I wrote Ada each day when I was in the military." I'm not sure when Mom and Dad began practicing the faith mentioned in Matthew 21, but what I observed and learned of their early lives demonstrated examples of living by faith. Pending challenges seemed bleak and uncertain for the young lovers, and the thought of not seeing each other regularly already weighed on their hearts. Dad was drafted into the service after Pearl Harbor, but he didn't leave for induction at Fort Snelling until March 1.

Chapter 3

Military Challenges

Don and Ada walking around New York

In October 1940, 17 million American men registered for the first peacetime draft in US history. Very likely, Dad's name appeared on that list. Women assisted the troops and worked 8-hour days, 6 days a week and earned a minimum pay of $0.78. Rosie the Riveter earned at least $40.56/week.

March 23, 2000, I provided a notebook for Dad to record military memories. I assumed writing would take his mind off his loneliness because Mom's situation prevented her from living with Dad in their apartment. His military comments quoted were found in that notebook. The newlyweds took advantage of unexpected opportunities to spend time together during Dad's military service.

"I was drafted into the service after Pearl Harbor, but I did not leave for the induction station [Fort Snelling] until March 1, 1942. I took an oath to serve my country," journaled the ex-military soldier. "Starting March 2, I spent about a week running errands until we shipped to Fort Bliss, Texas, for my 13 weeks of basic training."

More men were picked up in Davenport, Iowa, and Fort Leavenworth, Kansas, where he was assigned to 604th Battery B. "I was a Battery B man until I was discharged as a Staff Sergeant November 8, 1945," recalled Dad.

The newlyweds took advantage of unexpected opportunities to spend time together during military service.

Mom and Dad had received a red cow from her brother Gordy and mother Inger Larsen as a wedding gift. The newlyweds decided the bride should visit the groom in Texas as long as the cow money lasted. Ada rode the challenging bus ride by herself because the speed law had dropped to 35 mph to conserve gas and rubber, making the ride tedious. "It was a long trip from Minnesota to Texas," wrote Dad.

"We rented rooms for $5 per night. That helped extend our time together for nearly a month. We ate a lot of sour buttermilk, but it was good. She did stay in a guest house for a while."

Rain hadn't fallen until the men arrived in Texas on August 22, 1942, the day they received a Marching Order. Water was a foot deep when they had to load trucks onto the train in the desert with guns and other things. What a challenge! They loaded all their possessions onto two trains, mostly using flatbeds.

Portrait photo of Ada taken in New York.

"I stood guard on a flatbed with a 90-millimeter gun going across Texas. We passed by fields of huge watermelons," remembered watermelon-lover Don.

The train crew didn't know where they were headed because sealed orders directed them to the next destination, then a new crew took charge. The train crossed a 2-mile bridge over the Mississippi River at New Orleans.

Men traveled in coach cars, and the sound of the steam locomotive blowing its steam was etched in Don's memory after traveling through Birmingham, Alabama; Meridian, Mississippi; and on to Nashville, Tennessee. Ernie Hill, a good military friend of Don's, caught a card tossed by a young girl at the railroad station as they passed through Nashville. Ernie and the girl began corresponding, became happily married, and lived in Green Castle, Indiana, where Dad and Mom visited them in retirement times.

Finally, the military train arrived in Elizabeth, New Jersey, and the men were taken into the woods on Staten Island.

"There we pitched our pup tents for the night. This was nothing but a swamp between two truck gardens," Dad penned. "I eventually qualified for a Staff Sergeant ranking that brought a big increase in pay. I received $30 per month when I first began. Now I was up to $78 per month. $100 would be sent home to Ada." That was big money in those days.

Don & Ada (right) celebrated their 2nd wedding anniversary with friends Corporal Ed Grebenc and his wife at the Aquarium Restaurant, New York's largest seafood restaurant

"We were at the firing range. I believe it was September when I got an emergency call from home," recalled Dad. "Ada was in labor and had been taken to the hospital, and I could get an emergency furlough to go home. But I was 110 miles east of New York City and had no car to get back to headquarters. I started out hitch hiking back to pick up my furlough papers, etc. I rode most parts in a potato truck. At least, it moved in the right direction. I finally picked up the papers I had to have. Went to Grand Central Station to get a train for Minnesota at 4 p.m. I arrived in Tyler 18 hours later, with coal dust and dirt all over me."

"Tyler looked mighty small when we pulled into the station after living in New York with its skyscrapers and all. What a sad but happy reunion with Ada. We lost our firstborn, but I was home for 10 days. How short they were! The days just flew, and I was headed back to New York. Emergencies were the only things that made you eligible for furlough during war times."

The second Christmas (1943) Don got a 14-day furlough just before the holiday, so Ada rode the train back to New York with Don. She and a friend, Marie Muckala from Minnesota, got defense jobs working to build P.T. boats for the Navy. Later, Ada always told Don she helped make the P.T. boat President Kennedy had driven and nearly lost his life.

Reaching Times Square was a one-hour boat and train ride from the Norgaard's apartment on Staten Island. Don was able to get home quite often just before payday. He and Ada used to go on Don's pass when they enjoyed visiting Times Square and New York Central Railroad

Depot, just watching the many people coming and going. Some were happy and some were crying. Since it was war time, some had lost friends and family.

When Ada came to New York City by herself, Don met her at the Pennsylvania Hotel. He wrote that Ada was afraid she was going to get lost. "One little girl from the country," said Don. "I could have helped, but it didn't work. I think the girls at that time were braver than they are now."

Ada temporarily kept a 1943 diary of their experiences living in New York. When she worked on the PT boats, sometimes she would return from work to find her husband at the apartment. I imagine the couple's greetings during the unexpected visit were filled with love and excitement.

On February 18, Don couldn't leave base to spend time with Ada because the city was practicing a blackout. The next night she wrote, "Don came home for supper and the night. It was such a beautiful moonlight night, and we rode a ferry over to New York. Had lunch in New York. They had a blackout while we were in the lunchroom."

Ada's notes occasionally mentioned going to "the camp" to see Don, but she didn't mention how she traveled. We can't imagine what both did while staying in the New York area over 70 years ago during war time. They experienced living in Hackensack, New Jersey; Blackstone, Virginia; and Fayetteville, North Carolina, as well as Staten Island, N.J.

Ada ran both an electric drill and a screwdriver when she worked. One evening Don had supper ready. Chicken, mashed potatoes with gravy, and sliced tomatoes greeted her when she arrived home after a long day. He had also baked a "very good lemon pie" for dessert. They still had time to go shopping and to a show after eating.

Rumors afloat presented a challenge to motivate them making good use of spending their short time together.

"We got to see more of New York than we did before," remarked Don. "We took in a program at the Radio City Music Hall and saw a Christmas program there. It was just gorgeous. The orchestra came up out of the floor and many other odd things came to this little old country boy."

They also visited a science museum, Chinatown, and Macy's to see some of the balloon animals floating for the Macy's Thanksgiving Day Parade.

One day in January 1945, Don's unit received "move orders" to prepare for overseas. January 25, 1945, Battery B. arrived in Le Havre in France. Four battalions consolidated the kitchen equipment to feed more men more efficiently. They started a day's chow line at 10 a.m. and served until 2 p.m. One day the kitchen crew received a challenging notification at 9 a.m. They would be feeding 1,200 more men at noon since they were disembarking ships and had nothing to eat.

Mess Sergeant Don Norgaard supervised a mess hall and kitchen while in the army. Responsibilities included making daily menus, keeping daily ration records, supervising the cooks and mess attendants while preparing and serving food. He was also responsible for the discipline, sanitation and efficiency of the kitchen and mess hall. A cook prepared and cooked meats, vegetables, gravies, soups, salads and baked bread, rolls, cakes, pies and pastries besides setting up and operating a field range.

I found this information on a photocopy of Dad's Army of the United States Separation qualification record, dating November 8, 1945.

Don recorded both the good and the not-so-good experiences and challenges while Battery B moved its way through European countries. The U.S. troops were welcomed into Holland April 1. People told them how the German troops had come in and raided homes, taking bikes and whatever else they wanted. American soldiers were told they were the answer to the Dutch people's prayers. The next stop was Belgium where the men were surprised that the locals spoke fluent American English. Other locations Don and his buddies traveled through included France and the Eiffel Tower, Holland, Belgium, and Luxembourg.

Possibly the highlight of Don's time in Europe was when he received a diagnosis of why he suffered from a bad back that hadn't really slowed him down.

Chapter 4

Challenge of Back Injury Ends Military Duty

Three military generations: Don, his son-in-law C. Paul Thomason, and granddaughter Vanyse home on military leave for Christmas.

When Dad was reminiscing in 2000, he wrote about injuring his back and serving in the military with the pain. "All through the European travels my back had been bothering me. I hurt it in the states prior to embarking. I had made a high jump in Georgia for height tries. I was young enough to make one more try, and I landed on my tailbone. Not funny. I am still paying the price to this day." [2000] About March 1945 a hospital in Germany decided to send me to a General Hospital in France. It was there they discovered I had cracked a disk, so they decided to ship me stateside." This sounded encouraging to him. Dad recalled his experience returning home via crossing the ocean in a boat. "Our ship was docked at a small town on the English Chanel. I think we waited about 3 days to board it. Then we began to sail. We had white sheets to sleep on, breakfast served in bed. This had been a banana boat pre-war. We spent our days on deck, no shirts on. Live entertainment on board every night. Life couldn't be better. But of course, Ada couldn't enjoy this. Her time would come when we got home." It appears that Don's love for Ada was foremost on his mind.

Dad remembered his experience when arriving to his homeland. "What a wonderful sight New York was when being outside looking in. They sent several luxury cruisers out to meet us. Bands playing. They gave us doughnuts and coffee when we docked in New York. The first matter of business was a free phone call home, announcing our ship arrived in the USA. A well-known comedian put on a good live show for us."

Another high point of his life happened approximately August 8, 1946, when the military began gathering other patients like Don to send to the closest home general hospital. He left Halloran General Hospital on Staten Island for Springfield, Missouri, where he was examined in O-Reilly General Hospital and received a 30-day furlough after his injury was diagnosed as conditions of his back, right hip and right leg causing him 20% disability to his right hip and leg. He was eager to return home to Minnesota and didn't receive back surgery.

Free time in a park on Manhattan Island.

As I was a growing teen, I noticed Dad and Mom's monthly special event was when our mailman delivered a VA disability check.

Dad and two buddies received a three-day pass to New York City to help celebrate V.J. Day. He described this day in his memoir. "New York never had such a celebration. Several million people crowded into Times Square. You could not see anything but people as far as one could see. My two buddies and I held our hands so we wouldn't get separated, but we did, so when the other buddy and I passed the first Subway entrance, we managed to catch the subway to begin a way back to the hospital. I saw a woman fall, and the mob walked right over the top of her. I don't know if she was hurt or not. Thank God for bringing me through this experience."

Thinking back on his buddies, Dad wrote in his March 2000 journaling, "I believe I am one of the few buddies who are still working."

The next move was transferring to a hospital closer to home, but when he arrived in Tyler, he began farming at the Blomgren farm.

"WWII left a solid impression on America's WWII Generation," said Tom Brokaw in his book Our Finest Hour. He wrote that all veterans of WWII hold the American flag as an almost sacred symbol of patriotism. Many went on to promote a campaign to make desecration of the flag unconstitutional. Dad was one who supported that philosophy, even to the point of criticizing a brother-in-law who chose to wear a tie that appeared to have been an American flag.

Dwelling on military thoughts became history to Dad, after Val's husband and daughter served in the military. C. Paul Thomason grew up sixty miles north of Duluth in Finland, MN and served with the Marines in Viet Nam two tours from February 1968 until August 1969. He had attained the Marines' rank of Buck Sg. E5. The C. Paul Thomason family can thank Paul's military service in Viet Nam for meeting Val at a wedding in northern Minnesota on November 1, 1969. Val's girlfriend married a Viet Nam Marine friend of Paul that day. Six months later, May 6, 1970, Val and Paul's wedding took place in Tyler, and many Norgaard relatives and/or friends met Paul for the first time that day.

Don's granddaughter Vanyse showing off her girls Charlie & Piper in the navigator's seat of a C130.

Dad was thrilled later when he learned Val and Paul's daughter Vanyse enlisted into the MN Air National Guard (ANG). She is a busy woman who is still an active military person. Below, her story is told well in the paragraphs she wrote to me.

"I wanted to eventually be a pilot. I was also taking flying lessons during college, which was a challenge to balance my classes and to have a way to pay for them as well. I did not get commissioned right away, and it happened when I moved to the Wyoming ANG and was accepted as a navigator on C-130s. By this time, I had been deployed many times as a Loadmaster and had met my current husband. Shortly after we were married, I went to Officer Training School and then my navigator training, which encompassed most of the first two years of marriage.

"I then deployed right after my training. I was finally home with my husband, where we lived in Arizona. We had two girls, Piper and Charlee, within twenty-three months of each other. Life has been a rollercoaster ever since. I have had to leave my family many times, due to my military career. I was lucky enough to be able to have my husband's family living near Cheyenne and able to bring my girls with me, and able to have someone take care of them while I was at work in the Guard, which was my main job at the time, along with substitute teaching until the girls were both in school. Once both were attending school, I was fortunate enough to become a teacher at their school and have been balancing being a mom, wife, teacher and warrior (currently over 25 years), all at the same time."

Grandpa Norgaard would have been popping his military buttons if he were still living and keeping up with his granddaughter's military activities and advances. Piper and Charlee would have liked spending time with their great grandparents Don and Ada Norgaard.

Chapter 5

Farming Challenges: Growing Crops and Children

> **Don built the milking parlor, but the building around it came a few years later.**

Dad concluded his military memoir comments by writing, "When I got home [from the Springfield, Missouri hospital], I rented the Blomgren's 80 acres to farm the next year." By 1942, Myron and Jean Blomgren had moved from a farm northeast of Arco where Dad had worked for them. Now they resided at an acreage a short distance northeast of Tyler.

WWII was over, and Dad wasted no time getting back into farming. As a small child, I remember seeing him working Blomgren's farmland, including grain shocks a short walking distance from where Mom and Dad were renting a farm.

Dad and Mom were soon raising children on their rented farm. I was a Baby Boomer born November 3, 1946. Dad occasionally referred to this little girl as "my bundle of joy." Earlier the story mentioned Mom having a miscarriage and Dad had been called home from New York. There was also another miscarriage during WWII. I wonder if the stress of war caused the miscarriages because Mom was able to deliver four healthy babies after the war was over.

Jean Blomgren's poem included her perspective of Mom and Dad's new challenge.

They rented a farm and started a new life.

By Tyler they lived—a happy man and wife.

Their home then was blessed with laughter and joy by the arrival of three dear girls and one swell boy."

The farm Dad and Mom rented produced an abundance of fruit. Six pear trees, eight to ten apple trees and a few grape vines grew there. Several plum trees grew in the cow pasture. Mom was able to save money when it came time to preserve the plums and apples by canning them. Since the pear trees produced more fruit than Mom could use, she gave friends and neighbors some of the apples to use. Grape vines were productive the first years our family lived on the farm, but each year the grape vines would bear less and less until the vines died.

A house with three bedrooms and one bathroom between two of the bedrooms was more than adequate for the small family, but circumstances quickly changed. As a small child, I slept on a portable roll-away cot in the living room. Grandma Inger Larsen lived with us and had her own bedroom, Mom and Dad had theirs, and for several years the third bedroom was for a couple young men who were offered housing when they were hired to help Dad with farm work. When I was older, I was moved to Grandma Larsen's room to share her bed and room.

Baby Valerie was born November 12, 1949. I vividly remember the night of July 1, 1953, when I was sharing Grandma's bed. Dad knocked on the door to awaken us and tell me that I had a new baby sister named Wendy, but I cried because I was hoping for a baby brother. Wendy never let me forget that I cried when she was born. After Wendy's birth, Grandma Inger's conditions made life difficult for the growing family. Soon Grandma was moved to a senior care facility in Balaton, and I inherited her bedroom. I got my wish for a brother when David was born on August 9, 1957. While he and Mom were in the Tyler Hospital, Grandma Inger was admitted there for an injury from falling, but she passed away after Mom and David had been discharged and arrived home at the farm.

I remember vividly when family members and friends visited in our house after Grandma's funeral service. The house was packed with visitors while baby David slept quietly in a dark blue baby buggy parked along the outside wall in the corner of the dining room. Never heard a sound from my new little brother.

Mom soon taught me how to help her with baby David by spoon feeding him while he was tucked securely into a highchair. I learned how to change diapers, entertain the baby, and the list went on.

The small kitchen in our house didn't please Mom because several activities happened there all day. The kitchen had doors to the dining room, a bedroom, outdoors, and the basement. The four doors often created traffic congestions.

Dad never recovered from his back injury, and none of his children ever saw him stand tall and straight similar as his early military photos captured. He always slept on his side. As we children were getting older, we could help with farm-related work, so Dad no longer hired live-in helpers. When needed, Mom filled in by helping in the barn. She had grown up milking cows by hand, but she had milked the cows outdoors.

The old barn on the farm was in poor condition, and Dad wanted to expand his dairy cow herd, so the landlord built a new barn in 1949. **After the barn was finished, I rode to South St. Paul with Dad and Mom to buy some cattle. Since he had a large, efficient barn, he wanted more milk cows. As a result, he bought fourteen that day.** Formerly, he had milked 4 cows by hand while sitting on a one-legged wooden stool. The "new" barn had space for installing electric milking machines to make the farm chores much easier.

When Dad finished milking a cow, he poured the fresh milk into a cream separator. It is still a mystery to this writer how a cream separator works, and Dad tried explaining numerous times how the device worked. After I came home from school, a dreaded job of washing milk separator parts was waiting for me to wash the equipment before evening milking time.

I also got in Dad's way because I wanted to help. Later in life, Dad told me that I was especially interested when watching builders trowel the cement on the floor. Grandma Agnes Norgaard told me she had been followed by her little granddaughter asking questions when I was in her kitchen. One lasting piece of advice from Grandma Agnes dealt with using and washing sharp knives. I am still cautious when washing knives so there will be no injuries. The habit of asking questions has never left me, even though I am now the grandma.

Dad was patient with me when I was seven or eight while learning to ride my 2-wheel bike. Every time Dad adjusted the trainer wheels, when I didn't see him. He stood back to watch how well I could balance on the bike. One day he wanted to remove the trainer wheels, but I wouldn't let him. I NEEDED THOSE WHEELS! I insisted that the bike and I would end up in a heap on the gravel driveway without them. Dad heeded my demand and left the wheels on before telling me to take a ride. He stood back and laughed as I rode down the driveway in perfect balance. . . with the training wheels never touching the ground! He tried to convince me that I didn't need the wheels anymore, but I didn't believe him.

Finally, one day I let Dad remove the wheels. He held the bike while I mounted and started peddling away from him. It took just seconds for me to realize that Dad wasn't following along. I had graduated from training wheels because My patient dad stood back and laughed at my accomplishment.

Did my successful bike training signal Dad that his eight-year-old daughter could then drive a tractor? He had let me drive when I rode along on tractor rides, and he taught me how to disk, drag, and rake hay. It was fun for about three years; then I discovered I had more fun playing than helping Dad. I complained every time he asked for my help. One day Dad asked Val to help him instead of me. Gradually, the job became hers. She enjoyed helping and working outdoors more than I did. Dad trained Val to use the tractor for cultivating corn, something he didn't ask me to do.

Housework was more inviting for me than working outside. Mom taught me to cook and clean at an early age. A spice cake from a Betty Crocker cake mix box was my first project, and it turned out well. When David was born, I was nearly 10 ½ years old. Aunt Florence Larsen kept Val and Wendy, so they played with their cousins Kathy and Scott who were the same ages as their visiting cousins. Aunt May Dwire did the laundry. There wasn't much left for me to do while Mom was in the hospital. I wanted to cook Dad's meals, but Dad and I were invited out for meals most of the time, and once Dad took me out for supper. I remembered one noon when I was preparing Dad's meat and potato meal. He came into the house to eat, but rather than doing outside work, he helped with meal preparation before we could eat, Mom had started teaching me how to cook and clean at an early age.

A considerable amount of Dad's farmland was once a lake bottom; consequently, there was a big hill nearly a half mile long on the land. Whenever there was snow on the hill, Mom spent half an hour getting her daughters ready to go sliding on the hill, but sometimes they stayed outside for just fifteen minutes. The wetter we got, the

Don and Ada relaxed and were spectators of the farm auction.

more fun we had. Someone was always falling into the snow, and sliding was best if there was only a thin layer of snow over the dead grass. Numerous times friends or relatives would go sliding with us.

Mom and Dad continued their friendship with the Myron Blomgren family as neighbors. Dennis, Dean, and sometimes their friends from Tyler rode bikes to our farm. Knowing Dad's sense of humor, he probably stood back and laughed while watching industrious kids working hard to clear fallen tree limbs, trash, etc. from a grove that stretched along the north side of our house lawn. We were motivated to create a clear path for bike racing events, and then there's the winter when the gang moved into our unheated, rustic, dirt-floor basement to play a Monopoly game that never ended. Gradually, we sisters noticed that our game money was changing color, and we couldn't figure out what was causing the change. Sometime later, we discovered the solution—our friends had been smuggling game money from their home and hiding it under the table!

The Thorvald "Tut" Nielsen family lived just across the country gravel road between Norgaards and Blomgrens. I liked to cross the road to the Nielsen house, especially to plink on their beautiful upright grand piano. Dad and Mom bought the piano when the Nielsens were planning to move because the house they were moving into was too small for the large piano. I started playing piano when it found its new home in our living room. I began taking piano lessons immediately, so Dad and Mom decided to buy the piano for $25. I still appreciate my parents' decision at that time because I still play piano.

After moving to our next farm, we siblings occasionally fought for our turns playing the piano. At times Mom had to ask us to find something else to do. Several years later, this piano was moved to my St. Paul house for a few years, but the treasured instrument ended up in an Indiana home when Wendy's family followed Laurel's job to Indianapolis.

Every person in the Norgaard family had different characteristics, and Valerie and I had many good times together. Of course, like most sisters, we had our disagreements, usually a couple each day. If not, Mom wondered if we were feeling OK. When we were teens, she was amazed to discover that Val and I were sharing a book to read while in bed without any bickering. Wonders never cease!

Davie loved to sing. When he came home from Sunday School as a youngster, he taught his sisters the songs he had learned that day. The family could tell he did something wrong when his face looked guilty.

Davie had been a remarkably good talker starting as a youngster. When people came to visit, he climbed up on their laps and talked, even though it was the first time he might have seen the person.

Wendy was much like David in this respect. She also talked to complete strangers about anything that happened to enter her mind. She was four years older than Davie, so she should have outgrown this habit when he came along, but she never outgrew her desire to talk.

One of my worst faults was a bad temper. I could have earned greater respect from siblings if I wasn't so quick at losing my temper after Mom put me in charge. Sometimes I would hear from Val, "You're not the boss!" after Mom gave instructions or made corrections.

Grandma Agnes Norgaard was a special lady who would always have chocolate-covered mint candies to share with children. She had a reputation for being a good cook in the Tyler area and was kept busy prior to high school graduations, holidays, and other special events needing her delicious baked products. She was also our babysitter because we needed supervision when our parents were attending a meeting elsewhere.

Grandma Inger Larson was also a special person. She lived with the Norgaard family most of my live until I was about nine years old. I would frequently lie in bed at night and talk to her about her past, her sisters and brothers or her children: May Dwire, Agnes Johnson, Mom, and Gordon Larsen.

Chapter 6

Challenge of Buying a Farm

Aerial view of Don's first farm he rented.

Renting farmland wasn't the ideal dream Dad had envisioned when he dreamed of buying a place to call his own. For several years he was alert trying to find a farm with reasonable terms. There were Sunday afternoons when he would take the family for a car ride to areas unfamiliar to us children. Looking back on those times, I suspect that there was more to those rides than mere site seeing.

He may have used the drive to check out available farms. He later chose to buy the farm in the area where he had taken us on Sunday drives.

Dad agonized and fretted about making the right decision to buy his ideal farm on the market. I remember seeing him looking miserable while sitting at the kitchen table trying to make decisions. Finally, Dad's dream place entered the market, meaning good land, good location, and reasonable terms. He planned to pay $25,000 for the 260 acres by borrowing funds from the Production Credit Association (PCA).

Dad's farm of choice had more rundown buildings than the ones where we were currently living. Dilapidated buildings, including the house, had stood idle for five years, but Dad had plans for renovating the buildings.

View of the building sight Don bought.

The first time I saw the place Dad chose, I hated it. The buildings seemed more run down than the ones on the place the family was currently living. Dad didn't tell his children at the time that they would probably be going swimming by the farm site where his dad was born.

Dad purchased our future farm on the north side of the road across from Benton Lake in 1958. He began farming the land as soon as possible after purchasing it, however, the family didn't move to the building site until two years later. This circumstance presented a challenge to Mom and Dad because they had to transport the machinery eight miles from the current home to the new farm, and a lot of time and fuel were consumed. During the winter before moving, Dad had two accidents. When transporting sileage, he barely escaped death while traveling along a highway pulling a sileage wagon. He had a blow-out on a tractor tire, throwing the tractor and wagon into the road ditch. He just missed rolling the tractor over into a fifteen-foot drainage ditch. Fortunately, he wasn't injured. A couple weeks after this mishap, an icy road caused him to drive his car into the ditch, but he had no serious repercussions.

If fields weren't in good working conditions, Dad repaired buildings and accomplished much more work each day because he didn't need to drive home for a meal. For two years, Mom delivered meals from home to the new farm nearly every day, except Sunday. We children rode along if it wasn't a school day. David, a toddler, stood and leaned against his Mommy when riding in the car. The road crossed a railroad track at the bottom of a hill a few miles from the new farm. I have never forgotten Dad's

> *Don hadn't finished the bathroom in the new house, and a swarm of bees attacked him in the "outhouse." He quickly burned the unwanted building.*

wise comment about railroad crossings. When I approach a railroad crossing, I remember: "It's always train time at the railroad track."

Before moving to the new farm, Dad wanted to make numerous improvements on the buildings. Fixing the barn, a dark and dreary place for milking cows, topped his to-do list. After much thought, he decided to install a milking parlor. No longer would he find himself squeezed between the cows while milking, but in the parlor, cows' tails swished at his eye level if Dad didn't secure their tails to something stationary.

Milking cows in the parlor was entirely different than the stanchion system with which Dad had been familiar with for years. His milking parlor had just three stalls lined up, one in front of the other, and Dad. The stalls were elevated, so the work was done near shoulder height. Erecting something such as this building was not easy. Since Dad did all the major construction himself, building took longer than if a professional carpenter had done the work.

Because Dad didn't feel qualified to work on kitchen cupboards, they were the only renovation hired to be done. Removing the pantry/kitchen wall made room for cupboards. The result was a U-shaped, very efficient, small kitchen working area.

Running water was available to the house after the cupboards were installed and hard water was piped into the house. Before the kitchen sink was installed, only a small hand pump inside the house provided water. Digging a draining system was a long, laborious process. Dad did the work himself, but little David like to help his Daddy with the work.

Soft water wasn't a major problem because the cistern had been connected to another hand pump in the house. The only change needing to be done was rerouting the pipes. Soft water the first day after the family moved in was available inside the house.

Since the house had been vacant, a lot of cleaning needed to be done. Washing away dirt and filth topped the to-do list. Mom and Aunt Agnes spent numerous long hours removing grimy film from the interior surfaces.

They scrubbed several times before they could say the house was thoroughly cleaned.

Painting and papering were next on the list. All the walls downstairs needed papering. This project was accomplished shortly before moving day so the house wouldn't become dirty again. After Mom selected the wallpaper, Aunt Agnes and Aunt May helped her hang paper on the walls. They also papered one of the two upstairs bedrooms.

Ceilings in the living room and downstairs bedroom were covered with decorative tin, but no one liked tin at the time. Mom and Dad decided to paper the ceilings after taking the tin down, but they made one major mistake: hanging paper before heating the entire house. The new paper on the ceiling began slightly expanding.

This expansion was unnoticeable, but the paper cracked and tore. Damaged paper hung on the walls about a year. My perfectionist Dad, who didn't like to see cracked wallpaper, decided to install square ceiling tiles that contributed a great improvement to the room.

The house's white woodwork had yellowed with age, so all woodwork was repainted white before our family moved in. Varnish wore off the wood floors; consequently, Mom asked to have the floors varnished again.

A bedroom upstairs with two shades of blue walls was the only room in the house remaining the same. It wouldn't have been so bad, except the wall colors didn't match.

Finally, all the hard work had transformed the old house into a comfortable home for the family. More beneficial changes were made later.

February 22, 1960: Moving day finally arrived. The weather was cold, and I was disappointd I had to go to school instead of experiencing the excitement of moving. During the school day, my thoughts focused on riding a school bus when I knew only a half dozen of the kids living on that bus route. After a few months, I felt like I had known the kids all my life. Donna (a year older) and Marilyn (a year younger) became my bus friends. My dad was a friend of Marilyn's dad from the Battery B unit, so our dads had brought our families together.

When Val and I arrived home via the bus after school that day, all the furniture had been arranged in the house, and every room was amazingly transformed in just one day! I easily changed my original attitude of the house and realized how inviting it looked when furnished.

Like father, like son. Little David liked to help Daddy install the new bathroom.

The summer after we moved in, I helped paint our upstairs bedroom walls yellow and the woodwork white. I was barefooted while painting when I received a bee sting on the bottom of one foot. It hurt a lot, but Mom thought it was extremely funny. Her attitude was understandable because she had never been stung by a bee! The ceiling and part of the walls were covered with tin, and in the not-too-distant future, sheetrock was hung to replace the tin.

Bees continuing living in the walls startled mice and caused a ruckus when we least expected it. We would find dead bees on the floor beneath the windows, but somehow, we also discovered dead bees at the food of our bed between the two sheets.

Dad hadn't been looking forward to milking cows for the first time in the new milking parlor he had constructed. Not only would the cows be agitated from being moved, but the parlor was also new to them—anyone familiar with cattle knows that they are creatures of habit. Surprisingly, the milking process went smoothly the first time in the new unfamiliar facilities.

We girls, especially Val and I, considered it great fun living in a different house because we had an excuse for not putting away the washed and dried dishes. We didn't know where to put them! This tactic didn't work long since we soon decided where the dishes belonged.

Toddler Davie had a difficult time adjusting to the confusion of moving. He was merely 2 ½ years at the time, so he didn't understand what was happening and was ill for two days. After the living room floor was covered with a green-tone shag carpet, he started farming on the floor with his toy tractors and other miniature toy farm equipment. He didn't appreciate having an older sister vacuuming the carpet on cleaning day because the topography of the carpet was vacuumed away.

Occasionally after supper, Mom and Dad drove us to the lake for swimming during warm weather. We didn't need to do much coaxing to get Dad into the water. He was hesitant at first, but he enjoyed playing with us children in the water.

Swimming wasn't Dad's only water sport. He was eager to go fishing after he moved so close to the lake, but he didn't get to fish as often as he would have liked because farming responsibilities topped his priority list.

The main difference between the new home and the former one was that our home now had a second level story, even if there were only two rooms upstairs. The larger room was Val & Wendy's room, a much brighter room than mine, but I was satisfied having a room of my own. The stairway fit into a corner of my room floor, and everyone had to pass through to get to the other room. When Davie outgrew his crib downstairs in Mom and Dad's room, he was moved upstairs to share a room with Wendy, and Val moved into my room. One evening Mom checked on us because she heard no ruckus or arguing. The sisters surprised her when the oldest daughters lay in bed holding and reading the same library book!

One disadvantage of this house was the lack of a dining room; only the kitchen area was available for furniture from the former living and dining rooms. Two tables were in the kitchen area immediately after arrival. Mom, however, liked her new kitchen. The actual working area was compact and much smaller than in our former house, but she had more counter space. The area resembled a kitchenette, and the only problem was a crowded workspace when more than two people were working.

During Spring 1961, Dad accidently rolled his Allis Chalmers tractor and broke his arm while using the tractor loader in the farmyard. Mom and Dad said Val offered to do the work outside if I worked in the house. Of course, this choice was fine for both of us. Val was more willing to work outside for Dad than I was.

Dad and Mom Norgaard were always important to the lives of their children. He knew enough not to overwork himself: just about every day at noon He would lie down to rest, always lying on his side and have his head covered with a newspaper. "Just resting my eyes," he would say because of his back injury. The only exceptions were during the spring planting season or the fall harvest season.

Dad was an energetic man who would try to tackle a big task, like building wagons for use on his farm. Other things he made were a four-row cultivator and a four-row corn planter. He used stern discipline, but he wasn't too strict. He would take time off from his work to take us children where we wanted (needed) to go. He also gave us money without asking a long list of questions.

Mom, also energetic, didn't take time to rest unless almost all her work was done. Sometimes this habit wasn't good because she overworked herself. Then her nerves

Don injured his arm when the Allis Chalmers tractor rolled over.

were on edge, and even something minor could annoy her. The family still had a lot of fun with her when she sat down and played a game if the children had obeyed her.

Mom also sacrificed for the kids, but she wasn't quite as lenient as Dad when money was concerned. She wanted to know why money was needed.

When we girls walked up the farm driveway after the school bus dropped us off, Mom was walking across the farmyard carrying 5-gallon pails full of feed in both hands for the cows. The distance between the grain shed and the milking parlor wasn't far, but the pails were heavy. Seeing Mom working so hard convinced me I'd never marry a farmer. She would greet me with her supper instructions or tell me to decide what I wanted to cook. We had a lot of fun with her when she sat down and played a game if we children had been obeying her.

The statements about Dad & Mom's discipline and work were recorded in 1962 by me and supervised by Mom and Dad. (Carolyn Van Loh)

Chapter 7

Host and Hostess Activities

Don willingly carved turkey for guests.

Mom and Dad hosted a turkey dinner for Mom's Larsen siblings and their growing children each December 25. It wasn't unusual for Dad to help Mom, especially when it was time to carve the large roasted turkey. The number of guests increased as cousins often brought their future spouse, and as time passed, cousins also began bringing their growing small children. I enjoyed socializing with aunts, uncles, and cousins, and Mom and Dad welcomed every dinner guest.

Dad's brother Arnold, his wife Fern, and their children, two daughter and a son, were our New Year's Day guests to ring in the new year. Several winter memories with the Norgaard cousins included down hill sledding on one of the farms.

Mom and Dad's open hearts willingly reached out to friends and families, neighbors and occasionally out-of-town guests. Their reaching out to a new couple at Tyler's First Baptist Church ultimately resulted in a lifetime relationship. We children now consider the couple as one of our family. Let me tell you how I met them.

The Baptist church had an active youth program. During the December 1963 Christmas season, Pastor John Ballentine led the teens on a caroling activity one evening. He alerted the youth that one stop was the home of a chiropractor who had recently moved to Tyler and was living in a new house. I was surprised when a young man welcomed us at the door. In my mind, a doctor should be much older than this young man. Later, I found out Dr. Brian Williamson and his wife Judy were a mere ten years older than I was. When they became active in the Baptist church, they met the Norgaard family.

"We just clicked," remarked Judy. She said Don and Ada meant the world to their son and daughter, Todd and Lisa.

Mom and Dad soon developed their lasting relationship with the four Williamson family members. Dad was willing to help the chiropractor with challenging projects in his "new house"; Mom took Judy under her wings and both women enjoyed their times spent in the kitchen. Judy said Mom taught her how to make bread, lefse and other delicacies. Mom appreciated being able to talk with Judy about a variety of topics, including spiritual concerns. "It was nice," said Judy, for both couples to be active in Tyler's Baptist Church.

The age difference between the two women was conducive to a mother/daughter relationship. We children considered the Williamson family as unofficially adopted family members. When Brian and Judy's children needed a babysitter, teenagers Val and Wendy enjoyed the privilege of getting acquainted with the children while they had a chance to earn some spending money.

When I was living at home preparing for my wedding (June 1968), Judy graciously loaned me her bridal veil that had aged about 10 years, so she gave me permission to replace the netting. Two years later, Val wore this veil for her wedding, and another two years later Wendy wore it for her wedding.

Family friend Judy Williamson assisted Carolyn for her wedding.

Val, Wendy, and I lived in the Twin Cities during the 1970s. We siblings appreciated having Brian and Judy living close to Mom and Dad, especially for their willingness to assist Mom and Dad in their elderly years. Dad, on occasion after Mom's passing would think nothing of calling the Williamsons for help day or night when his children weren't available. Brian and Judy usually took Dad to church after he no longer owned a car, but when Brian left his earthly home for Glory in Heaven, Judy filled the gap.

When still living at home, Todd and Lisa thought the world of my parents and enjoyed visiting the farm, with or without their own mom and dad, and were greeted as grandchildren. Todd liked to shadow my dad around the farm, who showed and explained the various farm projects, including the milking parlor. When Todd was a youngster, he wanted to grow up and become a farmer. As he grew older, he was able to fill in needed job positions on the farm, but he later became an ordained minister, now serving in a Virginia, Minnesota, Baptist church. He had graduated from Pillsbury Baptist Bible College and studied at Central Seminary.

Visiting the farm with our own families was an event for us daughters, but the visit was an event for our parents as well. Val's daughter Vanyse expressed her thoughts on spending time with her grandparents.

She commented, "I was able to see first-hand the work ethics of my grandparents for many years. This affected me in how I view work and my responsibilities. I joined the MN Air National Guard while in college and had to take a year off to do it. Grandpa Don was ecstatic! For the first time he ever wrote me multi-page letters while I was in Basic Training. My military career and his time during WWII were mostly what we talked about when we saw each other once I joined. One Christmas we even wore our uniforms for a picture. Grandpa Don in his Army greens, my dad in his Marine greens, and myself in my AF Blues."

Mom and Dad graciously welcomed their future son/daughters-in-law when we children introduced a potential new family member. My marriage brought in another David, who grew up fifty miles away from Tyler in Westbrook; Val married C. Paul, who grew up in Minnesota's Arrowhead region; Wendy and David married local spouses Laurel Grenz and Pam Hansen who graduated from Tyler High School. Pam praised the loving way she was received during her relationship with her "in-laws." She asserted that she had won the lottery when her mother-in-law was Ada.

***

A big chest freezer conveniently sitting in Mom's kitchen was usually fully packed, and Dad was known to open the freezer lid while remarking, "We could not go to the store for a year and still not starve." Some of the contents were Mom's baked goods, some ice cream products delivered by Schwan's delivery truck, or meat products from the farm. Homemade pickles and other goods were stored in the dirt-floored basement of their house. The adjacent cemented storm cellar was ideal for potatoes and carrots grown in the farm's garden. We never needed to use the cellar for storm protection, but small creatures like mice managed to make a nest there. Later in life, I discovered Mom had hated mice. I had trapped mice as a small girl at our first home when she paid me a nickel for every mouse I caught and disposed of them.

Grandchildren were especially dear to Mom and were privileged to visit their Grandpa Norgaard's farm from time to time. Aaron Grenz remembers picking strawberries in the spring with his brother Micah. He said the strawberry patches seemed huge and were always filled with fresh berries that he and his brother Micah could pick. Grandma often served her visitors fresh strawberry sauce with half & half.

Mom liked to say, "It would be extra special to live long enough to be a great grandmother." That desire was fulfilled for her six times. Lily, Kenzie, Jake, Isaac Van Loh, Kaitlyn and Karsten Grenz were born. Mom received her wish and became a Great Grandma able to meet some of her "great" babies.

To say Wendy loved strawberries could be an "understatement." One weekend when Wendy and I were visiting, Mom was preparing two delicious strawberry pies and humorously talked about eating an entire pie. Wendy took the challenge, but Mom gave her an even greater challenge. She must eat a complete Sunday dinner before eating an entire pie, each piece topped with whipped topping. Wendy broke family records by eating the entire pie and survived with no problems!

Mom had a reputation for being a great cook. Harvesting crews, hunting crews, friends and family could count on outstanding meals and sweets like pies, caramel rolls and her outstanding ginger molasses rolled out and decorated cookies.

Family members arriving from a distance often looked forward to freshly baked caramel rolls, another of Mom's specialties waiting for her visitors. Since my husband Dave and I lived closer, when Mom learned we were stopping by for a visit, she, Dad, or both might bake a pie for coffee time. Sometimes it seemed Mom and Dad were trying to out-cook each other, but the results were good. Aaron also remembers having his grandpa's homemade spaghetti when the adults had oyster stew. Mom was a typical grandma who might spoil her grandchildren with high sugar cereals and served them several Schwan's ice cream products stored in the kitchen freezer.

Mom and Dad unhesitatingly opened their home to overnight guests, planned or spontaneous. My brother-in-law Paul and his wife Susan who was about seven months pregnant were invited to spend one night during a mission conference at the Baptist church; an unexpected snowstorm blocked them into the farm site a couple extra days. Dad, who had a humorous attitude, kidded Susan by saying he had assisted delivering babies for some of his milk cows and offered his delivery experience to Susan! She had plenty of time returning home to the MN Twin Cities before her daughter Sarah was born about six weeks later.

During one of my last years at home, Mom invited Myron & Jean Blomgren and their teenaged son Dean to our farm, despite a pending snowstorm after church one early April Sunday evening. The Blomgrens started home after lunch, but they quickly turned around and returned to the Norgaard farm because of stormy conditions. Everyone agreed the wisest decision was to stay overnight at our farm, and Jean agreed with the majority even though she had wanted desperately to fight the storm because she was up against a deadline at home. Yes, the storm was unusual for the month of April.

Dad's humor was rather low the next morning after he discovered cows had climbed over the usually electric fence recently covered with snow and were running loose in a blizzard. Some of the Norgaards and Blomgrens volunteered to brave the blizzard and joined an unplanned cattle roundup. I remember standing near Dad in the blizzard when I said, "Isn't it exciting to be rounding up cattle in a blizzard?"

I don't remember Dad's exact comment, but I know he was quite negative under the circumstances. After the storm decreased, the cows were safe again. I don't recall the exact time our guests left, but it was probably later in the day as soon as the roads opened.

Chapter 8

Vacations Cause Relaxation During the Challenging Times

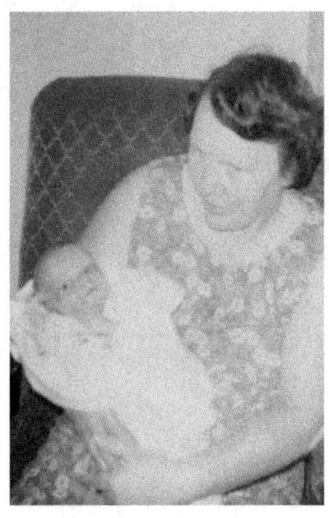

Ada met her first grandchild Tim Van Loh in Greenville, South Carolina.

Many fishing trips included Aunt May, Uncle Roy, and usually their sons Keith and Merlin to northern Minnesota. Dad and Uncle Roy were interested in the fishing, so a lodge upon a lake of choice was chosen. If the lake was considered good for fishing, Dad and Roy thought they also had a good place to stay. We kids didn't always appreciate the final decision because we judged a lake by its swimming beach. Sometimes their ideas on the ideal place to stay were exactly the opposite of their parents. Roy and Dad were usually victorious since the vacation was for their benefit. Everyone was happy a few times when a good swimming beach and a good lake for fishing were nearby.

Keith, two years older than this writer, commented on fishing trips, "One of my vivid memories was of 'The One That Got Away!' Don, Roy, and I would sometimes take the Ada & May 12-foot boat to some out-of-the-way lake to fish. I hooked into a 'really nice' northern (the prize species) using a red and white daredevil. Dad was running the motor and Don was getting the net. I should have played the northern out, but I got too exciting and reeled him right to the side of the boat. He twisted, turned, and broke the line before Don could get a net on him. No blame ever placed, but I know we all felt bad!"

Time moved on to distant places.

Soon after our June 1968 wedding, my husband Dave and I left Minnesota for Greenville, South Carolina and Bob Jones University. Two years later Mom and Dad's first grandchild, Timothy David, arrived. Dad drove Mom to the airport, and she eagerly flew to us by herself because she was excited to meet Timothy. Just having Mom with us was extra special for me. The following year, Mom and Dad traveled to South Carolina with Uncle Roy and Aunt May. Their itinerary included a trip via the Appalachian Train to the Washington, D.C. area to see the sights and drove to see one of Mom and May's cousins who lived a short distance away in Maryland. Our small Van Loh family followed the visitors with our '68 Dodge Dart as far as D.C. before heading back to our homes in Minnesota or South Carolina.

Mom returned to South Carolina in March 1972 when Daniel John, her second grandson, was born. The young Van Loh family moved to the Twin Cities later that year. Driving to/from southwestern Minnesota to the metropolitan Twin Cities was much more convenient than traveling halfway across the United States. Grandpa and Grandma could easily arrange to attend their grandchildren's school and church programs.

I was teaching at Bryant Ave. Christian School in SW Minneapolis, and Aaron Grenz was a kindergartener there who played the Gingerbread Man in a drama. After viewing a rehearsal, I called Mom and Dad to tell them about Aaron's role. They were able to leave behind our brother David to do the milking and other necessary farm work while they quickly prepared for their destination and must have surprised the Grenz family. They had probably packed their bags to stay overnight with them or possibly the Van Loh home—my memory is blurry, but Mom and Dad's devotion to grandchildren was demonstrated and remembered.

Dad and Mom's summer vacations between 1972-1997 focused on joining WWII Battery B men with their wives at vacation spots in Minnesota, Michigan, Virginia, Wisconsin, Missouri, Tennessee, North Carolina and Iowa, to name a few. Sometimes family members traveled with the soldiers, especially when Dad and Mom were aging and appreciated having younger people doing the driving. I remember a couple times my husband and I drove them to these reunions. We enjoyed meeting the men and their wives, but I regret not asking the retired soldiers questions about their military experiences. What a wealth of information I could have gleaned!

Dave and I remember attending the Battery B. Reunion in Greensboro, North Carolina, where Captain Keely and his wife lived. A gold-trimmed coffee mug sitting on a windowsill in my kitchen is a reminder of that trip. One side reads: 604th Battery "B", with a company logo. The other side reads: Battery "B" Reunion, Greensboro, N.C., August 1-2-3, 1975. A special perk for Dave and me was a side trip back to Greenville, South Carolina, where we had lived about four years.

When Wendy's family lived in Indianapolis or Chicago areas, Dad and Mom rode with the Van Loh family of four to those cities. Dad would comment on balls and other sports equipment his grandsons brought, and the grandsons commented on their grandpa taking up too much space sitting in the back seat. When the trips were scheduled for Thanksgiving, the women had a cookie making marathon and started Christmas shopping. Mom did well with the baking, but she needed to sit in a mall while the rest were facing the shopping crowd. Val and her hubby C. Paul Thomason and brother David and his wife Pam traveled to join in on the Grenz baking marathons and shopping.

Chapter 9

Challenge of Saying Good-bye to Farming

Empty barn behind auction buyers.

Mom and Dad remembered I turned my back on a farmwife's lifestyle when I left the farm after high school. Surprise! Eighteen years later, Dave and I accepted the challenge of leaving our SW Twin Cities home within walking distance of Minnehaha Creek. We moved to the Van Loh family farm near Westbrook because Dave's parents retired from farming and bought a house in town.

A big move for us was on June 21, 1982, our 14th wedding anniversary! By the way, I never regretted moving to become a farmwife of a farmer's son who began living on the farm when he was just two years old.

My parents didn't express their feelings or offer advice when Dave and I told them about our decision for me to become a farm wife. Less than a year after we started farming, they were forced to move from their farm.

Our move's timing was providential because a drive to Tyler from our farm took about an hour, visits were convenient, and later when Dad was adjusting to being a widower, I could try to encourage him and sometimes be his chauffeur to the VA Hospital in Sioux Falls. It was during this time when I urged Dad to write his military memoirs cited earlier in this book.

Dad had been contemplating to buy a farm and planned to pay $25,000 for the farm while he had begun renting since 1948. He agonized and fretted about the right decision to make about ten years later. I remember him sitting at the kitchen table looking miserable while making a decision. He might have neglected seeking sound advice about financing with Production Credit Association (PCA) for the 260 acres adjacent to the farm where his dad was born.

He invested countless hours as well as the money to make the farm he dreamed it to be. Dad's troubles began in 1980 when he expanded his dairy business by adding to his barn and his herd of cows, in addition to buying a new silo. Milk cows were selling for $2000.

"We were doubling the operation to support two families. You might say it was bad timing," Dad said in retrospect to a newspaper reporter. "When I borrowed the money, it looked like it would pencil out. Then interest rates went from 9 to 20 percent. It seemed strange that I had one year to come up with $64,000 when I paid only $25,000 for the farm when I bought it."

Prior to the foreclosure, he dealt with a farm disease spreading through the future milking calf pens, thus Dad faced another challenge.

He sold machinery and livestock to pay back his original $95,000 debt to PCA and tried to keep his farm, but the money was only enough to reduce the debt, not eliminate it.

Dad explained to a friend, "I had to go to a restaurant to find out they were foreclosing on me. It was in the paper, and someone told me about it. Six weeks later the sheriff delivered the official notice."

PCA didn't go completely through the terms of the loan agreement with him, but Dad blamed himself for the oversight. "That was my own fault because I didn't read the back page. But I've never known where PCA will read the back page and that's where the teeth are."

Dad was not alone in his financial situation because the crisis was nation-wide in the early 1980s. His challenge was devastating, but he kept his eyes on God and the truth of Matthew 21:21-22 as cited in the Introduction. His faith was strong.

Dad had a machinery and livestock auction on the farm to pay his original $95,000 debt to PCA and trying to keep his farm, but the money earned was enough to reduce the debt only, not eliminate it.

Rev. Wayne Anderson, Dad's pastor at Tyler's First Baptist Church during the farm crisis, was with Dad when the county sheriff served the foreclosure papers. "I remember life's testimony Don was when his farm was foreclosed upon. The sheriff came to serve papers, and Dad was sitting at the table preparing his Sunday School lesson. The sheriff apologized for what he had to do. He calmly said, 'That's OK. You need to do what you have to do.' The sheriff was amazed."

Rev. Anderson and his wife Sharon stood with Dad on the steps of the Lincoln Court House in Ivanhoe, Minnesota, during the scheduled public foreclosure auction. The area outside the courthouse was alive with spectators, primarily people representing protest organizations like American Agriculture Movement (AAM), Citizens Organization Acting Together (COACT), and National Farmers Organization (NFO) waved their protesting signs.

The decade of the '80s saw the demise of numerous farms because of adverse financial circumstances. Interest rates grew rapidly, exceeding 20 percent at one point. Farmers were unable to repay their loans and were forced to sell out. Less fortunate ones lost their farms through foreclosure by their lending institutions. Dad was one such farmer. PCA in Minnesota had completed foreclosures involving 16 farms the previous year.

The foreclosure challenge was devastating, but Dad kept his eyes on God and valued the truth of Matthew 21:21,22 as cited in the introduction. His faith was strong. Uncertain what the future held, he continued teaching the teen boys Sunday School class at First Baptist Church.

Dale Steenhoven, one of his teen students from 64-68, said, "I thank God for his influence on my life. I wish I would have listened more closely." Dale continued his Bible study at Pillsbury Baptist Bible College and Central Seminary, both in Minnesota. He is currently the pastor of Will County Baptist Temple in Joliet, Illinois. Don treasured a letter of apology he received from Dale after he was a pastor.

When national television news teams covered Mom and Dad's story of losing their farm, they started receiving heart-felt letters from sympathizers, most of whom sent small donations. The excerpts below were found in letters Mom saved after receiving them from different states.

"I want to express my sympathy for the loss of your farm. It made me cry to see how well you expressed your feeling at losing a lifetime of work."

"We cannot afford to help financially, but we do wish you well and hope that the fruits of your labor pay off. We sympathize with your situation and remember you in our prayers."

"My heart went out to you upon hearing about your recent foreclosure. Although I am not a farmer, I have been in small business most of my life and know the hard times that most of you are experiencing. Keep your faith in the Lord Jesus Christ, for through him all things are possible."

"Dear Ada & Don. We watched the news tonight and were astonished to see Don on the selling of your farm. My heart aches for you in these troubled times. We will pray that something good will come out of this. Love, [military buddy]"

"Who I am is unimportant. A gift to be given without recognition. This is not charity. It is a gift of love, concern, and compassion for my fellow man. God bless you and your loved ones."

Mom saved the notes received from across the USA like these cited above. The kind words, primarily from unknown people, soothed my parents in an unexpected, but comforting way.

Chapter 10

Life After Farming

Don and Ada the lucky winner of the Tyler Kiwanis raffle fundraiser.

Dave and Kathy Guida, who lived a couple miles north on the road Mom and Dad had originally lived on. The Guida couple was more than happy to invite Mom and Dad to live in a trailer home standing empty on their farm site. "It seemed the thing to do," said David G concerning the retired couple who had lost their farm on which Dad had worked so hard and made numerous improvements.

"We had a very special time when Don and Ada lived with us on our farm," said David Guida. Dad quickly caught his interest in birds like bobwhites, a bird whose chirping sound can easily be imitated by their care givers who liked to carry on a "conversation" with a bobwhite. Dave laughingly told of his experience when he thought he was chirping back and forth with the bird. Alas, he was chirping like a bird when he walked around the house and saw Dad chirping like a bird while painting window frames on Guida's house. The two men had been chirping to each other and enjoyed life in the process.

When I was talking with Dave about his family's experience of having Mom and Dad living on their farm, he described Mom as a nanny. She walked up a short hill from the trailer house where they lived to the Guida home and supervised the children while their parents were busy elsewhere. Mom loved small children and willingly cared for the Guida children still in diapers. When she had time, she also washed the family's laundry and prepared a meal to have ready when Kathy came home from work. Knowing Mom was an avid reader, I'm assuming she read books to the children as she spent time with them.

Dad must have noticed the Guida field crops and animal farm needing additional hired help. On occasion, he would ask Dave if he needed more help. Dad may have met a potential worker looking for a job while talking with people at the Tyler Baptist church, and he thought of the Guida farm.

Mom and Dad adjusted to a lifestyle not dependent on an agricultural yearly cycle. Dad declared he didn't want to be a substitute worker for a farmer in the dairy business. He soon created a new definition for the common term "Happy Hour." He had never participated in the usual Happy Hour, but he may have set his body clock to allow him to roll over and go back to sleep. No longer was he required to rise before the sun seven days a week, regardless of bitter cold temperature, rain, snow, or sleep waiting to greet him. After the farm auction, Dad did carpenter work and painting jobs. He had plenty of opportunities perfecting these skills when he improved his own farm buildings and "started from scratch" by erecting new structures.

After a busy day, Mom occupied her time while resting, plus reading her Bible and novels. More than once she earned recognition for her participation in the Minnesota Baptist reading competitions. (My Grandma Agnes Norgaard had also earned similar reading recognition.) When Dad was no longer farming, he didn't want to sit still. His desire to work with the soil never left him, so gardening was his delight. Raising beautiful flowers and delicious vegetables was an enjoyable pastime. Young Todd Williamson, who accompanied Dad while he was working, observed that farming was always fun and not a job for my dad, and not a struggle or hard work. He saw a man happy with what he was doing.

One project Dad enjoyed was working with flower beds around the Tyler hospital/nursing home. He took great pride in watching the colorful blossoms as they enhanced the greenery around the buildings. For a while Dad also hired out for painting jobs. Some were relatively easy, but other times he worked dangerously on an extension ladder. One time he overheard a comment from a spectator, "Get that old man off the ladder." I don't recall if that comment reminded Dad that it was time for him to quit painting, but it was time to find a safer pastime.

Retiring from being a dairy farmer freed him from being tied to his farm. Wendy and Laurel had been living in the Twin Cities area since their marriage in 1972, making it easy to assist with and get acquainted with grandsons Aaron (1975) and Micah (1976). Laurel's occupation led him to a job in Indianapolis he couldn't resist in 1981, so Wendy's stipulation for agreeing to the move was being able to return to the Minnesota family farm every Christmas. Snow tried preventing them one year, but our brother David met and carried the family a mile or two on his snowmobile because a road was blocked.

Since Dad was no longer tied to his farm morning and night, he and Mom drove to Indianapolis to contribute time and effort to the Grenz newly constructed home in 1985. With Dad's construction experiences, he had never laid bricks, but learned that job when he built a fireplace for Wendy and Laurel's new home.

Determining the time to break all ties with a farming environment may have come to Dad personally because no one I asked was able to explain when Mom and Dad chose to move into a government housing apartment in Tyler. They may have sensed their days on the Guida farm were nearly finished. They spent several comfortable years living in a 2-bedroom ground level New Vista apartment in the USDA Farmers Home Administration housing development along Highway 14 in Tyler. The original lease was dated June 15, 1992.

While living close to today's Tyler Avera Medical Group facility, Dad was pleased to work inside as a handy man and outside as a gardener in the flower beds around the building. The gardening job was a part of his working under the Green Thumb program. In May 1996 he was honored at the Sunrise Manor Nursing home in recognition for being a Green Thumb and receiving a certificate and a plant; these opportunities kept him busy a few years, even when Mom was a patient at the facility.

Some of the grandchildren may remember a story about Mom winning a drawing for a 1975 Cadillac Eldorado with a raffle conducted by the Tyler Kiwanis Club in 1997. Proceeds in excess of $3,500 were used to establish the Therkel Jorgensen Scholarship Fund at RTR High School. No memorable stories of Mom or Dad driving the Cadillac never happened with the car.

Dad had always been a talker; he once said he wouldn't make a hermit. He and Mom sometimes ate out with family and/or friends, but he was known to turn away from the table to see if anyone he knew was entering the dining room; it didn't matter if the small café was local or along the way on a road trip. I once saw Dad conversing with a woman while we were waiting to be seated at a restaurant in Marshall MN. When I asked who he had been talking with, he said he noticed the woman was wearing an Elkton, S.D., jacket. That stimulated him to strike up a conversation with a stranger.

Mom and Dad continued cooking and entertaining guests in the privacy of their apartment until August 2001 when Mom's death prompted Dad to move to Danebod Village where he had a small apartment and ate with all the residents three times a day. The important reason for his last move was socializing with other residents and helping whenever he had a chance.

Chapter 11

The Single Life

Don's Christmas card, taken in the Danebod lounge.

When Mom spent her last days in the hospital or nursing home, Dad was lonely and uncomfortable not wanting to live alone in their apartment surrounded by memories he had shared with Mom.

They were an avid life-long table game couple. As a child my bedroom was adjacent to the living room when we resided NE of Tyler. Mom and Dad set up a folding table in the living room and sometimes played one game of checkers lasting all evening—Mom was quick to make her checker moves, but Dad considered all the options, so his turn took much longer than Mom's. No matter how long Dad spent, Mom was usually the winner. The next morning, I would ask who won the checker game and heard the same answer: Mom.

In later years they switched to card games like Uno or Skip-o. Again, Mom often ended as the winner. Backgammon was another game they often played. In this game, shaking the dice before moving the game pieces determined the result, so success could depend on the dice throw rather than the entire game depending on making wise moves. Playing the Backgammon game gradually spread to family members participating when they came to visit.

It's easy to understand when Dad became a widower that he had difficulty filling his time in the evening. Television didn't meet his needs, and he also wasn't an ardent reader; simply knowing there was another person in the apartment comforted Dad. I slept a few nights in his apartment before he moved to Danebod congregate living, but I don't recall filling in as a table game partner.

After Mom's death, he moved into Danebod Village where he enjoyed the social life for nearly six years. He loved the meals (after adding hot sauce!), loved the fellowship with other residents, and loved having chores like clearing dishes from tables or watering outdoor plants around the village. Even though when he lived in congregate Danebod Village after Mom's death, Dad still missed her close companionship.

I remember "A day to remember" as Dad put it Dad January 26, 2022. After **Mom's death,** I had promised to drive him to Marshall at least once a month for a visit with Uncle Gordy and Aunt Florence. I was busy teaching at Westbrook, MN Immanuel Baptist Christian School, and the promise had slipped to the back of my mind. Early in the morning, I was awakened by my bedside phone ringing. Guess what? I wasn't very excited to change my plans for the day, but the time spent with Dad became a special day for me, too; Uncle Gordy, Mom's Larsen family historian, had some photo albums and a large box waiting to be perused when Dad and I arrived. Our historian even had a story to tell with each photo!

On our drive back to Tyler, Dad gave a continual commentary on the countryside as I drove down State Highway 19 to the county road that brought us to Tyler. I learned where 3-mile Creek was, although I didn't learn what it was three miles from. I also learned where Moonshine Valley was. Need I say more? Other times when I had driven Dad to destinations in various directions, he often pointed out a rural location where he had worked when he was a teen. Seeing the sites led to other history lessons, especially about people who had lived there.

The hug and kiss I received as I left Dad's apartment that day were all the thanks I needed. My drive back to Westbrook passed quickly because I had so many thoughts running through my head. I was bringing home a treasure more sentimental and valuable than treasures in the box Gordy gave me. I had learned several new stories of Dad and our family history, and I knew I had to print them into the computer before they were lost in the clutter of my mind.

I learned Dad cherished one-on-one times with his children. Several times he intimated his regrets for not being the attentive, affectionate dad he thought he should have been.

My brother Dave's farm employment sometimes prevented him from spending time with Dad. I arranged my schedule so I could share my time with Dad, especially after we children determined he should no longer drive a car. For one thing, we took turns driving Dad to his VA checkup appointments in Sioux Falls.

Dad's faith in God kept him going during his earthly life. He could rejoice that his wife of over fifty years was walking streets of gold in Heaven. He enjoyed life, and he took great pleasure in saying things that would get a laugh out of his listeners.

Older age did not prevent him from attending scheduled church services. Since he was no longer a licensed driver, church friends like Brian and Judy Williamson were willing to provide a ride to the Baptist church in Lake Benton. The Tyler church had merged with the Lake Benton church shortly after Mom passed away.

Dedication of the WWII Monument occurred on May 29, 2004, so Paul Thomason planned an itinerary that included taking Dad to our nation's capital for Dad to view the new monument honoring the soldiers who died in action and those still living, like Dad. Flying to Washington, D.C. must have been Dad's highlight experience while living as a widower. Son-in-law Paul volunteered to act as tour guide from Minneapolis/St. Paul (MSP) airport to Washington D.C,'s Regan airport. They visited other historic monuments in the mall area besides the recently built WWII memorial along the National Mall.

Excerpts printed below from a set of Dad's handwritten note cards describe his adventure that he used for an oral presentation to Tyler's American Legion members.

Wednesday, July 7, 2004—left Tyler. Stayed at Val's in Anoka and left Minneapolis with Paul by plane. I marvel at this plane's traveling smooth as silk seven miles above earth. Took a little over two hours for 2000 miles. I must have shown my driver's license three or four times before I ever got a seat to sit in. <u>Security</u>.

July 9—I hope we can find some transportation today when we start seeing the sights. I walked my legs off yesterday, but there are several conveyances available. Paul is going to check them out.

I am amazed by transportation in Washington. Much of it is underground railroad. We chose a ride for all day so we could get to all places of interest. Passengers could get on and off whenever they desired. Worked out well.

The WWII Memorial was everything as great you saw on television. I bought a sweatshirt with a WWII Veteran logo on it. It was quite a thrill to have total strangers come up and thank me for being in a world war. We saw the WWII Veterans Memorial on Saturday, July 10. I am at a loss of words to describe the experience.

I met many people who came up to pat me on my back and say thanks for serving. I said, 'I thank God for that'. They weren't all old people. Some were neat young chicks. It was a heart-felt experience. Ones who should have been thanking are long gone from this world when I discussed experiences with many vets. It made me feel like a big shot compared to them. There was no vet from a draft, like I did. We took training at Fort Bliss instead of waiting in reserve at the bulge. We fought in it.

Sunday, July 11—I'm sitting here in a Washington airport waiting for my plane to take off. What a relief this is after the endless trek to catch mass movers. All of them have been built since I was here in the middle '60s when I was traveling with Farm Bureau members to the big meetings we had with men like Senators.

I am glad Paul is here to pick the right one. If I had to do it, I'd never see Minnesota again. There are many tourists here. All in a hurry. I enjoyed every minute of the trip. It will be a big relief to settle on the plane here. I could have never done it without Paul, and I could never have been able to do so much walking if I hadn't done the fitness center every day back home. That is the best money I ever spent. Don't come here if you can't walk. Have a young brain since things are very confusing.

In summary to his American Legion audience, Dad said the following.

It was entertaining. The first question I'm asked is what did you see? I say I don't have years left in my life to tell them. I bet you don't have the patience to listen. Come up to my apartment at 9:30 a.m. or 2:30 p.m. to have a cup of coffee with me. We [Danebod] have very good coffee and the best goodies there; I'll be looking forward to seeing you. You need to see the site for yourself, but don't wait until you are old and retired.

When Dad mentioned most of the historical sites and memorials, he seemed grateful for his long life of 80+ years. He would comment on the "Thousands who have been killed in wars in the history of our nation." He mentioned numerous memorials erected as a reminder of our nation's founders, such as the Roosevelt and Kennedy memorials, men who had governed during his lifetime.

Knowing Dad, I'm thinking that he wouldn't have enjoyed his Washington, D.C. trip as much if he needed to leave Mom at home while he traveled. He would have thought of his dear wife of over 50 years who wasn't able to see the sights. This trip certainly filled a portion of the big gap in his life; starting when he learned about the trip and anticipated traveling by air and going to a destination he had toured earlier in his life

Chapter 12

Good-bye to This Earth

| *Don & Ada* |

Let not your heart be troubled; ye believe in God, believe also in me. In my Father's house are many mansions: if it were not so, I would have told you. I go to prepare a place for you. And if I go and prepare a place for you, I will come again and receive you unto myself; that where I am, there ye may be also. John 14: 1-4 (KJV)

Mom Departs from this Earth

Jesus was comforting his disciples when he spoke the John 14 words. Mom and Dad did not know the day, nor the hour, when God would call them home to Heaven where God had their mansions prepared. Mom's call was first. Tyler's ambulance attendants came to their apartment to help her up and transfer her to the Tyler hospital after she had fallen. Her last earthly days were spent between a hospital bed and a room in the local nursing home attached to the hospital.

She had been diabetic several years and was also treated for some other medical conditions when multiple myeloma blood cancer was detected shortly before she left her earthly life. Doctors wanted her to submit to kidney dialysis, but she didn't want to end a good life being controlled by the dreaded dialysis routine. Our family learned that Mom's days were numbered, and the number was few. Shortly after refusing dialysis and battling declining health, she was able to talk with friends and family visiting her in the hospital or calling her on the telephone, as far away as her grandson Tim who called from his home in Japan. Nearly every special friend and relative of Mom were able to talk to her for one last time.

Not knowing how soon Mom was departing for Heaven, I had promised to bring her a piece of pecan or lemon meringue pie when I said good-bye before driving to a church meeting in Owatona, but early the next morning, August 8, 2001, I received a cell phone call telling me Mom would soon be in Heaven. I immediately left for Tyler before my brother Dave called to tell me Mom had taken her last breath. I still think of Mom when I choose to eat one of the promised pie flavors. God's providential timing in calling Mom to Heaven spared her from living through the infamous 9-11 tragic series of events.

Dad Joins Mom in Glory

Dad called March 31, 1997, "D Day" for a short surgery to remove small growths from his bladder. He received bladder cancer treatment with chemo treatments at the Sioux Falls Veterans hospital and won the six-week battle over cancer tumors. He chuckled about his body being radioactive during the treatments before returned to his Tyler residence.

Eating a burger with a thick slice of onion from the Log Cabin, a small café across Highway 14 from Danebod Village, was one of Dad's favorite foods. The cafe called it the "Don burger". The evening of April 27, 2007, he was unable to find someone to enjoy an evening meal with him at the Log Cabin, but since he was determined to eat the burger, he started out on foot. Somehow, he fell or tripped on the curb of the highway and broke his hip. A phone call from my brother David told me what had happened, so I hopped into my car, drove to the VA hospital in Sioux Falls and slept on a chair in the lounge near Dad's room.

We children, a few grandchildren and two babies— great granddaughter Ada Grace and great grandson Ethan Hartung were recently adopted by granddaughter Ashley and her husband Jason Hartung—were visitors. When our son Dan visited his grandpa a day after surgery, his greeting included a comment saying, "Grandpa, Tim and I did not climb up a silo and stand on the top." Grandpa's response was priceless when he abruptly turned his head with a look of unbelief on his face. He may have been facing death, but his mind was sharp because he remembered the on-going chat he had with the two oldest grandsons.

Grandson Tim also had an opportunity to say good-bye to Grandpa shortly before the end. He asked, "Grandpa, what would you like me to say about your life?"

Dad's matter of fact response was simple. "I accepted Jesus Christ as my personal Savior, and I will go to Heaven."

"Grandpa, is there anything else?" asked Tim.

"There isn't anything else," Grandpa answered with assurance.

Rev. Tim Van Loh later officiated for the memorial service.

A couple days after Dad's fall, hip surgery was progressing well, but by Tuesday, pneumonia set in. We children were called in by the VA personnel because death was near. Son David spent a short time with his dad until he left to help with spring fieldwork. We three daughters were standing around Dad's hospital bed with a nurse when he quietly slipped away from earthly life about 1 a.m. on May 8, 2007. David and the coroner were called to the hospital.

We children were included in a special VA transfer to the morgue two stories lower than the room we were in. Dad was placed on a gurney and covered with a large Americana Flag. David guided the gurney from the front while I was pushing at the back. Val, Wendy and a nurse followed me. Wendy abruptly stopped the procession when we came to a large photo of the flag raising at Iwo Jima. She took a picture of Dad in front of the picture to show his love for the flag and the time spent in the military. What a memorable dignified experience at 2 a.m.!

Mom and Dad Welcome Wendy to Glory

Mom and Dad were spared of saying a final earthly good-bye to one of their dying children when Wendy succumbed to her battle with cancer, but they may have been the first of Heaven's residents to welcome her. She was diagnosed with breast cancer in 2005 and battled cancer until bone cancer ended her life in 2019. David and his wife Pam had visited Wendy the previous week, but Val and I were at her bedside on the morning of February 1, 2019, just a few minutes before God called her home to Heaven.

Wendy had claimed Matthew 11:28, "Come unto me all ye that labor and are heavy laden and I will give you rest." She penned, "I know that no one is promised a tomorrow so that our times are in God's hands." She wrote this sentence when she was discussing her faith in God's plans for her.

Wendy's daughter-in-law Gretchen, Micah's wife, delivered a eulogy for Wendy's funeral service: "Joy was one of her favorite words. She was an awesome grandmother building blanket forts, doing puzzles, painting rocks, baking, and remembering each of her grandchildren's favorite treats. Micah and I lived with Wendy and Laurel for two and a half years, and I can honestly say it was a wonderful time being together."

Gretchen concluded her eulogy with the following words and Scripture verses.

"My lips will shout for joy when I sing praises to you; my soul also, which you have redeemed." Psalm 71:23. Wendy was shouting for joy. Everyone was watching. We were learning from her. Even her grandchildren. She had so many people praying and watching and learning, and she taught us about our Father until the very end."

"The LORD is my strength and my shield; my heart trusts in him, and I am helped. My heart leaps for joy, and I will give thanks to him in song" (Psalm 28:7). Anyone who knew Wendy saw this thought in her and could observe the Holly Spirit living in her life. 'God is good. We are blessed.'"

Chapter 13

The Family Continues to Grow

Don and Ada bought the holiday meal celebrating their wedding anniversary and Ada's birthday. Dave, Val, Don, Ada, Carolyn and Wendy.

Mom and Dad enjoyed having their grandchildren visit them. My son Tim rode with his Aunt Wendy and future Uncle Laurel from St. Paul to visit Grandpa Norgaard's farm. He and his baby brother Dan were the only grandchildren at the time, so he was privileged to have Grandpa Don and Grandma Ada's undivided attention. I wonder how Tim's grandparents developed a special relationship to a two-year-old who wasn't familiar with them. It worked, as I recall.

Twenty years later, Grandpa wrote a letter for Tim to read on the plane while flying to Japan in the summer of 1995. Usually, Mom was the letter writer of the couple; but Dad's letters were few and far between. "I had been informed by my offspring I had never talked about myself. You are as much to blame for this as I am. You see, when you were little, you could care less listening to an old man. I was a grandpa who was too busy working and earning money to keep the farming operation going financially than to stand around talking. Kids, it's my hope each one of my grandchildren will receive a copy of this. If I get this one finished, I may write a follow-up chapter. I am sorry my spelling and English could stand some improvement. Blame that on to old age. I am 79 years old."

"From March 1, 1941, following our marriage on December 25, 1941, until November 8, 1945, was spent in the army. That is another story by itself. Tim, you are now a man. Let's just pretend that I am sitting in the seat there beside you. We are 30,000 feet high and traveling over 500 miles per hour. As man-to-man, Tim, I know just how you feel at this moment. You had to leave her standing there for now. You are close to tears. Let them flow. That is God's way of easing sorrow. You will be serving the Lord."

"You are already counting the time until she will be with you in Japan. Oh, what a happy reunion that will be. I know the feeling. Your grandmother and I had a number of those times while in the Service. The part when I left her in Tyler standing by the train depot after the furlough—we waved at each other as the train began moving slowly at first, then faster. Each puff of the steam locomotive taking us farther apart."

Finally, he concluded his writing. "I have never revealed much about my history to you in the younger generation. Partly because we have always been too busy to pass the word along, and partly because you get tired of listening to us 'old fogies.' Now I got you. I know you won't jump out of the plane. Someday we old Gramps will be in eternity and can no longer talk. So here goes."

Tim and Naomi, his wife, planned to teach English for Japanese at all ages. Tim began by teaching in public schools and later changed to a local medical school. Naomi developed her own methods of teaching English to adults. One approach both Tim and Naomi used included Bible studies. John Telloyan, Naomi's brother, has continued the pastoral leadership of a Gospel church that Tim organized and led until he, Naomi, Lily and Isaac moved to Minnesota early in the 21st Century.

Vanyse, five years younger than Tim, quickly learned to hold her own with four boy cousins, two older and two about the same age. From her perspective, she shared experiences they had at the farm.

"For a long time, I (Vanyse) was Grandpa and Grandma Norgaard's only granddaughter. I thought I was pretty darn special because of it and was treated quite special, too, by the whole family. I hung with the boy cousins as best I could, and according to the eight mm films for me picking on them, I even made them cry when I stole their balloons! We still talk about it to this day. I miss getting together every Christmas, even battling snowstorms, to get to the farm to see everybody. I did at time get relegated to girl activities. This didn't always make me happy, but I learned how to cross stitch and help in the kitchen."

She later learned to play by interacting with her only female cousin. "As I got older, one day I was no longer the only granddaughter in the family.

Don and Ada were privileged with eight grandchildren. One boy arrived later after this photo was taken.

My little blond-haired cousin Ashley appeared. She was pretty cute, and I didn't mind sharing the spotlight with her. We didn't always get to see each other, but she was my cousin and I like to think that she looked up to me a bit when I was around to visit. My grandparents were very generous, and I was able to bring my childhood friend to visit them on the farm in the summers for a week or more at a time. It was the best! I wouldn't trade the time spent at the farm for anything in the world. Picking strawberries from the big gardens and the kittens and helping milk cows on occasion—things I wish my own daughters had the opportunity to do."

Ashley and Zach, David's children, lived closer to their grandparents than any of their Norgaard cousins, and their grandparents were often available to fulfill childcare responsibilities. Looking back on the time spent together, Ashley commented on spending time with her grandparents, "It was a blessing. I could tell they cared for my soul and my future. Grandpa liked doing jokes, but Grandma was more serious."

Grandma Ada taught Ashley cooking and baking skills in the kitchen while Zachary spent time working with Grandpa Don in his Tyler apartment garden and working with the greenery around Tyler's hospital, a responsibility Grandpa enjoyed doing.

Ashley and her husband, Jason Hartung, experienced several miscarriages, so they adopted Ethan and Ada Grace close together. Ada Grace is named after both maternal great grandmothers: Ada Norgaard, Ashley's grandmother, and Grace Hartung, Jason's grandmother. "Both grandparents had a big part in who we became," remarked Ashley. "God has had a hand in it all."

The Hartung family is the largest of Mom and Dad's grandchildren's families. Ashley gave birth to Emi when negotiations were being made to adopt Anya, so the two girls are nearly twins in age. In addition to Emi's birth to Ashley and Jason, the Hartung family has been blessed with six adopted children from Ada Grace and Ethan, the oldest ones, to Imani, the youngest.

My son Dan and his wife live in a suburb of Minnesota's Twin Cities. Daughter Katherine is close to finishing high school, while McKenzie and her husband Ethan as well as son Jacob and his wife Lauren live in the NE Metro area.

Some of Mom and Dad's grandchildren moved from Minnesota. Val's daughter Vanyse resides in Arizona with her husband Gary Snow and two daughters; Wendy's husband Laurel, his sons Aaron and Micah, and their families live nearby to Laurel in Tennessee. Tim Van Loh, his wife Naomi, son Isaac will marry Brook soon, and daughter Lily with her husband Alex live in Michigan.

Ashley Hartung and Zach Norgaard are the only grandchildren who live near the southwest area of Minnesota where their Grandpa and Grandma Norgaard lived. Mom and Dad's extended family has increased to 51 members, with potential for another generation in the family.

If Dad were still living, he would have been pleased with Vanyse's currant military experience. When Ashley was asked what her Norgaard grandparents would think about the large Hartung family, she replied, "Grandma may have been concerned because we had taken no more than we could handle, but they would be approving the six adoptions."

During the 2020 Covid virus pandemic, great granddaughter McKenzie married Ethan Hale late in May at a Minnesota Bible Camp where they had met each other. The list of names, because of Covid virus regulations, didn't include either of her grandparents. Granddaughter Lily married Alex in their Lansing, Michigan, church parking lot in mid-October that year. Her dad Tim escorted her by riding in a red convertible to the outdoor altar/steps. Jacob and Lauren moved their wedding date from February 2021 to October 9, 2021, because of continuing Covid virus regulations. Many extended family members witnessed the ceremony and appreciated a delicious buffet of goodies.

Val's son Chad and his family experienced a battle with the Covid virus early in the pandemic, but they were able to participate in their 2021 downhill ski sporting events in Winter 2021.

Grandchildren have faced life's mountains quite different than what their grandparents faced in their lifetimes. Teachers adapted to various teaching methods. They faced major challenges when they were mandated to use distance learning to fulfill their teacher responsibilities. The strong faith in God that Mom and Dad depended on during their lifetimes is evident in great granddaughter Ashley's family with her husband Jason, a minister of the Gospel in two rural churches. Grandson Tim is Outreach Minister on a church staff in Lasing, Michigan. These two have lived their lives by putting their faith in God as did their Norgaard grandparents. Dan Van Loh practices as a family law attorney and uses biblical principles when counseling his clients. Other grandchildren face challenges unknown to their grandparents.

Chapter 14

Family Heritage

| *Chris and Inger Larsen (6/26/1907)* |

This section lays the foundation of the Ada (Larsen)/Don Norgaard family since their ancestors moved to southwestern Minnesota from European countries. Keep in mind these people faced challenges in their day without all the amenities people today depend on—electricity, cell phones, email/Facebook, radio/television news sources, and various transportation options. When reading this section, try to visualize facing challenging experiences cited in the following historical family story over a century ago.

Ada Lucille Larsen Norgaard

Ada was born December 24, 1917, close to WWI/Spanish influenza pandemic, on the Larsen family farm northeast of Arco in southwestern Minnesota. Her dad was Jens Christian "Chris" (b.1874, d.1935); her mom was Inger (Johnson) Larsen (b.1878, d.1957). On May 31, 1883, Chris, four siblings, and her parents Peter and Bodell Larson, left Holbeck, Denmark, for America. Chris' parents had drained all their savings after a serious illness. Their overwhelming challenge was trying to support their growing farm family.

The Larsen family arrived in New York June 17, 1883, and reached Marshall, Minnesota, on June 20, 1883. They settled on a farm with a log cabin near an uncle's farm. A bachelor living in a dugout hadn't followed Homestead Act regulations for the 60-acre farm south of Minneota, Minnesota. The Larsen family paid $125 for the property where Chris grew up. In 1885 his parents bought an installment plan for a cow, team of oxen and some chickens. They eventually built a house, and Bodell gave birth to five more babies, giving the family a total of 10 children.

The Tidemand Jensen and Marit Torsdatter Gansager Klevgaard family left Norway for America between 1864 and 1869. They changed the family name to Johnson. Four children traveled with them, and Inger, born in 1878, was the youngest of four Johnson children born in America.

The Johnson family lived temporarily in Blue Earth, Minnesota, before they bought a farm three miles south of Minneota and resided there the rest of their lives. Their challenges began when Tidemand was killed in a grain binder accident in 1885, and his wife Marit stepped up to the challenge of doing numerous farm chores in addition to housework. She died thirty-two years later.

When Chris herded cattle in his pasture, the neighbor girl Inger also herded cattle nearby. Chris later told his children that he and Inger took time to swim in a nearby creek. Inger claimed they were only wading together.

News of a gold discovery in Alaska spread in 1897. Chris, his brother Andrew, and three other men from the area headed to the Klondike gold fields, a real challenging mountain to face. According to one resource, Chris was the only one who took on the challenge of gold fields. One of the SW Minnesotans died; Chris' brother Andrew and the other two men returned to Marshall within a year.

Chris never got rich in Alaska, but he was satisfied with his mining adventure. He returned home in 1905. An article in the December 15, 1905, Minneota Masco carried a story of the Klondike challenge. The trip to Alaska and reaching Dawson City from the coast took fifteen months and required carrying two years' provisions. During the summer months, travel was impossible because the snow melted and made sleighing the only means of locomotion. Chris remained in Dawson City six years and traveled 1,100 miles farther up the Yukon River, where he spent some time before returning home. He worked in mining nearly all the time he was in Alaska and managed to gather enough of the gold metal to reimburse him well for the trip.

After returning to southwest Minnesota, Chris' challenge was farming on land he rented near his parents when he was a bachelor; he married Inger Larsen June 26, 1907. Their daughter May was born there in 1910. When the couple bought a farm near Arco, three more children were born: Agnes (1913), Ada (1917) and Gordon (1920).

Uncle Gordy once commented on the challenge of being the youngest of four children. "I always did feel kinda sorry for myself having to grow up with three big sisters. I say it was a miracle I grew up at all, but my sisters don't agree with me." I wonder if Uncle Gordy was a good mentor to his nephew David, Don and Ada's only son and younger than his three sisters.

A fire destroyed Dawson, Alaska, including all evidence of Chris' years there. Later, Gordon was determined to research his dad's Alaskan trip in the SW Minnesota State University (SMSU) library, using all local news articles of the trip. Gordon did the research, and asked Aunt May's daughter Sharen Sannerud and her sister-in-law Oda, Mrs. Bob Dwire, to take him to the library. Uncle Gordy left the SMSU library with photocopies of all the area newspaper stories filed there. Knowing my interest in history and writing, he gave me his set of article copies and asked me to type them. What a challenging experience! I had to read copies of antiquated newspapers, but the work was worth the effort.

I once received a phone call from an ecstatic Uncle Gordy. In the late 1900s/early 2000, he had seen a centennial commemorative story about Alaska gold mining in a Twin Cities Sunday paper. A photo containing a dozen or so gold miners spanned the width of the page, but names of the men weren't included. When Gordy showed me the photo, he asked if the man in the center back was his dad. Grandpa Larsen had died more than ten years before I was born, so I had never seen him, but the man in the photo certainly was like other photos I had seen. We both were thrilled to know we had the proof of Grandpa's stay in Alaska.

Donald Brodson Norgaard

Dad was born November 28, 1918, to Brodson (b. 1892, d. 1959) and Agnes Nicholls (b. 1899, d. 1973) Norgaard at their farm on the north side of Lake Benton, a brief walk from the lake's island. Dad's brother Arnold Bryant was born in 1921. A thorough family history of Grandma Agnes Nicholls' family is not available, but the family of ten children moved frequently because their father's job as a painter demanded he move from place to place. When I had the opportunity to see a Nicholls family tree as a young adult, I noticed each child had been born in a different location/state.

Agnes was born to Edward and Adele Nicholls in Lynch/Boyd(?), Nebraska in 1899. Family tradition states Samuel F.B. Morse (b.1791, d. 1822) was in Agnes' maternal grandmother's family tree. An unnamed Sir Nicholls, supposedly assumed to be a family member, had a part in purchasing Manhattan Island from Indian tribes in 1626. The unsettled lifestyle must have been challenging to my great grandparents Edward and Adele.

Dad once shared with me a remembrance of a childhood time during his Grandma Adele's visit to his home. Word came that her husband Edward was on his way. Dad chuckled as he shared about his Grandma

Nicholls quickly "hightailing it out of there" when she learned her husband would soon arrive at the Norgaard farm.

The first two wives of Kristen Hansen Norgaard (b.1851) died of tuberculosis in Denmark, and he was challenged to raise their three children. His first in-laws had financed his farming, but because of challenging economic conditions, he had gone bankrupt while farming. He immigrated alone from Denmark to America in 1882, but he earned money in Chicago for the passage of his children to America one at a time. His first job in the USA was stirring soap in the Kirk Soap factory, and he also had a milk delivery route in Chicago with delivery carriages named "Hansen's Dairy."

About 1882, 16-year-old Hansine Nelsen Meyer emigrated from Denmark to America. She settled in Chicago and met her future husband, Kristen Hansen Norgaard, when he delivered milk door-to-door. A widower with three children, Kris had a reputation of being a hard man with a bad temper, but that didn't stop Hansine. After they married, they owned a delicatessen store with their home in the same building. Hansine was just nineteen when she married Kristen, and she treated her three stepchildren as if they were her own. She spoke both Danish and German because she had been required to attend a German school when living in Denmark.

Kristen no doubt heard about an effort to acquire land by the Danish Evangelical Lutheran Church in America by bargaining for land from the railroads. In 1884, a committee of the church group convened at Clinton, Iowa, to find land where Danish immigrants could settle. An agreement was made with Winona and St. Peter Railroad Company to reserve 35,000 acres of land in Minnesota's southern Lincoln County (included land in Marshfield and Diamond Lake Township north of Lake Benton) for Danish Lutherans in and around Tyler. Kristen arrived in Tyler March 23, 1892, with his money and more from a few of his Chicago friends. He bought a farm on the northern edge of the Lake near Lake Benton, including the island. Land sold for $5 and $8 an acre.

A small cabin was the only house on the farm Kristen purchased. At the last minute, he decided to make the cabin more presentable before Hansine arrived from North Chicago. He was whitewashing the interior, so he sent his friend Henrick Ries to the train station five miles away at Tyler to meet his seven-month pregnant wife, their six children, all the farm equipment and a "marvelous" set of horses he had purchased.

Compared to their comfortable North Chicago home, Hansine and all the children cried when they saw the condition of their new home. The cabin didn't have room for everyone, so the first step was to build a lean-to on the cabin. Don's dad, Brodsen, was born in the cabin August 7, 1892, soon after his mother and siblings settled on the farm with Kris, a purebred Shorthorn breeder. Hansine and some of the children lived with a neighboring farmer for a couple weeks until the log cabin was ready for the entire family.

Esther Sorensen-Larsen, a niece of Brodsen, remembered when her uncle and Agnes were dating in Sidney, Montana, where they lived. Sidney was a Danish community opened to homesteading.

"When my Uncle Brodsen came to Montana, he made his home with my folks as did my Uncle Art, Jens, Johannes and Aunt Annie when they were out there. The boys all had farm jobs in the summer. Uncle Brodsen was the only one who found his future wife there. She made the first fruit salad I had ever tasted. Was it good! She brought green grapes, bananas and apples. I can't remember what else. Uncle Brodsen had a Maxwell Roadster. He would bring his girlfriend out to our place on Sundays.

"My Uncle and his girlfriend Agnes would go into the new parlor and sit on the davenport. They shut the door and my mother wouldn't let us kids be in there. We just couldn't understand why they wanted to be alone when they could have our company. We would go out to the porch and peek through the window. My uncle would sit and laugh at us. He had a good sense of humor and played with us a lot. We thought he was just tops."

*(Information found in "I Remember" by
Esther Sorensen-Larsen)*

On January 28, 1918, Brodsen and Agnes were married by Danish Lutheran Minister, Rev. Knutson, in Marshfield Township of Lincoln County, Minnesota. Donald was born to the couple in the same area on Thanksgiving Day, November 28, 1920.

Brodson and Agnes (1/28/1918)

Author's Biography

Carolyn Van Loh, 75, a retired English teacher, lives on the family farm less than 20 miles from the site of Laura Ingalls' family dugout along Plum Creek. She is an author, freelance writer, speaker and retired English teacher. Much of her writing focuses on history.

Education:

- Graduated from Tyler (MN)High School as a Baby Boomer in 1964
- Attended Pillsbury Baptist Bible College two years before transferring to Mankato State College and earned a B. S. degree March 1968.
- Master of Education in English from Clemson University Dec. 1971

Teaching opportunities:

- English at Bob Jones University 1 ½ years.
- Graduate Assistant at Clemson University 2 ½ years.
- Bryant Ave. Christian (9 yrs) and Westbrook Christian Day Schools (20yrs).
- English Professor at Pillsbury Baptist Bible College 4 ½ years.
- On-Line teacher/mentor.

- Summary: Carolyn Van Loh had been an active teacher most of her adult life.

Writing Career:

- Edited SW MN Farmer (1 yr) and Sentinel Tribune (2 ½ yrs)
- Freelanced for Sentinel Tribune, The Land, The Sailor, Tracy Headlight Herald.

Published 3 books:

- Strong Roots: the people of the MN Farm Bureau (2008; updated 2019)
- Great Is Thy Faithfulness (50-yr history of Pillsbury College) 2007
- A Place of Interest (John/Betty Van Loh family story) 2013.
- Ten articles focused on Cottonwood County history published on MNOPEDIA through the Minnesota Historical Society.
- Consulting opportunities and tutoring for writers asking for her advice.
- Has also assisted local high school English teachers.

www.ingramcontent.com/pod-product-compliance
Lightning Source LLC
LaVergne TN
LVHW011958070526
838202LV00054B/4958